# CHAPTER O

**Woodhouse, Far End, Baslow. 24th October, 1713**

Silence had greeted us as we followed the coffin into Church. It was packed, every pew taken, mourners standing in the aisles. People had come from far and wide. How did John know so many? What has happened? It has all gone so quickly and now I need time to think, be quiet, and yes, to grieve. How can I do this when I have all my eight children at home? I am a widow aged thirty six. My dear, darling husband has gone.

It is dusk and I am standing outside our old thatched house. It has been such a dismal day in every sense. The only sounds I can hear are the rooks circling as they settle to roost for the night in the wood behind and, just audible, the quiet trickle of the nearby stream. I shiver. In a minute I will go in and see my children; the little ones should already be in bed and the older ones tidying up the house after the day's sad events - enough of this wallowing in self-pity. There are plans to be made, new routines, if possible. John has been ill, on and off, for nearly a year and I am so very tired, especially as I am still nursing my youngest child, William, not yet a year old.

Elizabeth and Catherine are still helping Jess, who looks after the children, to get the young ones to bed and have given them warm milk to drink in front of the parlour fire. Often the children squabble, but not today. John's youngest brother, Christopher, still lives with us and has brought in logs which are stacked by the inglenook. Elizabeth and Catherine adore their uncle. Although he is twenty four I am now so glad he has not yet married and left home. There were times, I confess, I minded him being here but he looks after the farm and I could not have managed without him in the past few months. His mother died here upstairs giving him birth. This is his home.

Eventually I creep upstairs. This is a rambling old house and I try not to step on creaking boards. The eldest children have their own rooms, but when I peep in at my son Chris, who always looks so undernourished, his bed is empty and he has crept in to the truckle bed in the room of his younger brother, Johannes. Chris is thirteen and his bigger, younger brother, always to be found in the smithy workshop, is eleven. In the next room, seven years old Tommy is fast asleep. In the nursery are three little cots for five years old Ann, two years old Maria, sucking her thumb, and baby William.

I climb into bed, the bed I have shared with my husband for eighteen eventful years. It engulfs me. I weep a little and finally drift off to sleep dreaming of how we first met nearly twenty years ago.

# CHAPTER TWO

**Edensor in the summer of 1693**

Anna and Kate Greensmith had been sent by their father, Joshua, to look at the sheep on Calton pastures. Rumours were that a boundary wall had been vandalised and other stock was on their grazing. Josh and his son Edward were too busy to go as they had decided on a new method of abstracting lead that day and were all set up for it.

The sisters, Anna aged sixteen and Kate, fourteen, had been told that they need not hurry back but they were to keep to the usual track, not to venture near the building works of Chatsworth House and be sure to be back by four o clock. They would hear the distant church clock which chimed on the hour. They were very happy girls as they set off from their home in Pilsley in the pony and trap with the picnic their mother had given them. It was a beautiful day. Their brother Edward was a few years older than them, married to Elizabeth. They had a brood of children and lived in the nearby village of Edensor. Edward worked alongside his father extracting lead and copper from the surrounding hills. As they idled along Anna hoped that they could sort out the problem they had been sent to investigate, but how could they remove any stray sheep and how could they repair the stone wall? She was beginning to feel very stupid. When they reached the Calton boundary wall they unhitched the trap, tethered the pony on a longish rope to let it graze and walked all alongside the wall looking for damage. There only seemed to be the odd fallen small stone, nothing major. It was a long wall; by the time they had returned to the pony they were exhausted and flopped down on the grass to eat their food. Eventually they decided to return home. It seemed they had been sent on a wild goose chase but they had enjoyed the day of freedom, sunshine and girlish dreams.

There was an almighty explosion! The pony bolted, the two girls were almost flung out of the trap backwards. They were frightened. Their grandfather had told them about the cannons fired during the civil war but that was a long time ago. As the pony slowed down Anna managed to catch hold of the broken reigns; they were now already back nearly as far as Edensor, at least they could see the church spire. The distressed pony was all winded and lathered up so they decided to stop for a while before finding water. Anyway, the sun was still quite high in the sky and it would probably only take another half hour, if that, to reach home.

A horse was approaching. They thought they'd best be on their way home. As he approached them the rider dismounted.

"Are you alright?" he called. "I heard the blast and then saw your pony had taken off at great speed. Is your pony alright? It needs water. I was working on the gates in the Park when I needed to return to my forge in Edensor. I'm on my way there now." The girls had little time to recover any composure after the incident. He was laughing. "Come, I will lead you to the water trough."

That was the first time she had seen him. Anna instantly forgot her annoyance with her father for sending them on a needless journey. She later understood that the explosion was the first time the Greensmiths had used gun powder to loosen the ore which made the process of extraction with hand tools easier.

The lead was then smelted out of the ore in wood fired hearths on the hills.

At this time there was huge activity at Chatsworth House. Bess of Hardwick had built the beautiful property with her second husband Sir William Cavendish and few alterations had been made until 1686 when the 4th Earl began to pull down the South Front. His intention was to only alter this part of the house but he found building such an enjoyable project that he could not stop. The East Front followed, then new outbuildings, followed by grand formal gardens. All this work brought an influx of labour to the area together with artisans from France, Italy and Holland.

The two storey chapel in the south west corner had been started in 1688 and completed a few years later. In 1694 local residents were invited to view; the Greensmith sisters begged their parents to take them. They were not disappointed. It was all so richly decorated. There was cedar panelling with lime wood carvings, and a sumptuous Baroque alabaster reredos. Anna and Kate were totally in awe of the wonderful paintings on the walls and ceilings: scenes from the life of Christ by Laguerre and Ricard. Verrio had painted "Doubting Thomas" over the altar. The four black marble columns had been hewn from a single block quarried on Sheldon Moor a few miles away.

Anna and Kate could not possibly have known then how much their lives were to change. Unsophisticated they may have been but they were very inquisitive. They wanted to know about the craftsmen and the strange speaking artists. Little did the girls realize that their Derbyshire dialect was very strange indeed to visitors from afar! However, this did not detract from their natural beauty nor did it discourage the admiring glances of the craftsmen who, despite the language difficulties, were eager to converse, with the aid of local man, Samuel Watson. At first the Greensmith family thought he was rather retiring, but once he knew their interest was captured he proved to be helpful and most knowledgeable. Josh and his wife, Martha, immediately felt comfortable in the company of the man, whom they guessed was about their own age, or perhaps a year or two younger. He was well built and comfortably rounded, like themselves, full faced with brown eyes and his brown hair greying at the temples. His movements were unhurried and deliberate. Seeing how in awe her daughters were and how eager she was to widen their cultural interests, Martha suggested to Mr Watson that he might like to bring his wife along to their home the coming Sunday and share their meal.

"Thank you, Mrs Greensmith. I have no wife, but may I come alone?" he replied.

And so began their friendship on that coming Sunday and continued for many more Sundays to come. The two sisters were so impressed with what they had seen that day in the chapel at Chatsworth House, not just the vividly coloured paintings and exquisite carvings, but the artists themselves. They talked about it for days. There had been so much to see. They wanted to know more, where had the materials come from, how did the artists mix the colours, where did they get their inspiration? This was a new world to them.

"Please call me Sam. What is it you would like to know first?" he asked during the wonderful meal of spit-roasted leg of lamb (their own, of course).

Josh answered his new friend by saying perhaps Sam could tell them a little bit about himself to begin with. They already knew that he was a local man from the village of Heanor, a few miles away. He revealed: "I was fortunate enough to be a pupil of the carver Mr Charles Oakey in the parish of St Martin's in the fields. I also worked under the London carver Thomas Young for the Earl of Exeter at Burghley House and for George Vernon at Sudbury Hall and had many opportunities to study the fine work of Grinling Gibbons. I then returned to Derbyshire and was working alongside Thomas Young at Chatsworth, and we were later joined by Joel Lobb and his assistant William Davis. Last year Young left and Davis and I were both working as Lobb's assistants. Other carvers, including Nadauld and Cibber, came and went. Following a dispute over pay last year, the Earl dismissed his architect, John Talman, together with most of his London and foreign craftsmen, but I was kept on and rose to become principal carver. As well as carving I assist Sir Christopher Wren with independent valuations of the work done by Talman's team."

"Did you really carve the reredos in the chapel?" ventured Kate. "Oh yes," replied Sam "but it was designed by my master at the time, Cibber. He and I worked closely together and learnt much about one another. As he was away from home and my being a bachelor with no family ties I had time for him. He was the son of a Danish royal cabinet maker and travelled to Italy with a grant from Frederik III of Denmark and there studied classical art. He arrived in London around 1655 and joined the Long Acre workshop of John Stone. Initially, Cibber worked as a journeyman and then foreman to Stone. When Stone suffered paralysis he ran his master's workshop until the death of Stone in 1667. Cibber then set up business on his own. His independent career flourished when he was soon appointed a member of the Royal Household and a sculptor to the King. He realised his best opportunities lay in the City of London where, as you know, rebuilding was under way following the Great Fire. Then his career went from strength to strength." Sam paused to take a drink. Realizing his ale was all consumed Josh replenished the thirsty man's tankard. "He was gainfully employed and overcame a few financial hiccups."

"Does he have any family?" asked Martha.

"Well, yes" continued Sam. "Cibber was married twice, but told me little of his first wife. I gather that in 1670, whilst living in Bloomsbury, he married an heiress from Rutland, Jane Colley, who 'had 6000 pounds fortune.' Some of this was set aside for their three children. Cibber admitted to me that he gambled away the rest of his wife's fortune and then complicated his senior years by being imprisoned twice for debt and then having to reassert his standing with the Crown in order to continue to work."

The girls had never heard such a tale. They implored Sam to carry on.

"Eventually he won his first public contract, a large carving in relief for the memorial monument commemorating the Great Fire. This brought him into contact with Sir Christopher Wren, Surveyor of the King's Works. The sculptor was given day release from the Southwark debtors' prison to carve the ambitious tableau portraying the King as the kind force controlling the rebuilding programme. By all accounts this work was well paid and then more successful commissions followed. It may be of interest to you, Josh, that Cibber has been experimenting with lead sculpture which seems to be coming popular for formal gardens, as well as his stone figures so favourable with the aristocracy. Most likely his success is down to the fact that he is prepared to travel to their country estates and to economise by using local materials."

Martha would not allow Sam to say another word until he had had time to swallow his last mouthfuls of meat and eat some of the lovely apples and berries she had cooked.

After they left the table and were comfortably seated by the fire Sam carried on with his narrative: "Cibber's association with Wren was renewed with more work and he then moved on here to Chatsworth, which, of course was how and when I met him. As well as the major involvement with the alabaster reredos his work included the marble statues for the great staircase and the magnificent stone triton and sea-horses fountain. I understand that when he left here he was appointed Sculptor-in-Ordinary to William III in succession to Peter Besnier and he was also employed to repair statues in the Queen's Garden."

Sam admitted he wasn't so well informed about the other artists, but told the two girls he would tell them as much as he could on another occasion, if he might be permitted to come again. For now he was happy to finish his drink and then wend his way back to his lodgings in Edensor.

When the lovely gentleman had left them, the girls and their parents agreed they had enjoyed Sam's visit so very much and hoped he would come again. And that soon came to pass. Martha decided she would make her special game hot pot, for which she was well known. "You're going to a lot of trouble, wife!" Josh could see the big iron pot hanging from the chimney sway and the most delicious aroma percolating through the house.

Sam was expected that day and Josh noticed that his wife, still quite comely, had also gone to a lot of trouble with her appearance. Surely that couldn't be a new dress she was wearing? But that shade of cerulean really suited her and emphasised the blue of her eyes. Can't have this, he muttered to himself, better smarten myself up.

"I thought we would eat first, Sam, and then perhaps you would like to tell us more about your fellow artisans." Martha wanted everyone to appreciate the trouble she had gone to and perhaps enjoy some praise for her efforts before he got going!

The family remembered that the walls and ceilings in the Chapel were painted by Louis Laguerre and depict the image of Christ healing the sick. Sam was able to tell them that Laguerre was born in 1663 in Versailles, a godson of Louis XI, no less. He specialised in historical paintings which can be seen on walls and ceilings at Blenheim, Marlborough, Petworth, and Sudbury as well as Chatsworth where he had been working for a couple of years since 1692. Much of his work was done under the supervision of Antonio Verrio. At Chatsworth Laguerre also painted murals in the Hall showing scenes from the life of the Roman leader Julius Caesar.

Verrio was 'another kettle of fish altogether' and had made it very clear that he was keen to meet the girls. Fortunately, as far as Josh was concerned, there hadn't been time on the visitors' day and, furthermore, he did not want to encourage a social visit from him! None the less, his talent could not be disputed and he had already spent a year at Chatsworth from the autumn of 1691 then returned when the chapel was finished to see what progress had been made. Sam told them that Verrio, an Italian, was born in 1636 and married Massenzia Tornese. They had two sons and then moved to Naples. Apparently he worked in Florence, Rome and Genoa before moving to Toulouse in France. Sam carried on to say that when Verrio moved to Toulouse he seemed to have abandoned his family, was living as a libertine and during his short time at Chatsworth had shown himself to be a womaniser! (Ah, so Josh was right). But to return to his time in France, he eventually settled down with Francoise Dangley, an artist, and their son, Jean Baptiste was born. In about 1670 he moved to Paris and made many important contacts to further his career. He was a very prolific artist and became the protégée of Ralph Montagu (later 1st Duke of Montague), who introduced him to his first English patron, Henry Bennett, Earl of Arlington. Verrio's successful debut in London led to many other commissions from Royalty and the Nobility. He was so busy that it seems amazing that he managed to spend any time at all at Chatsworth. However, the ceiling in the long gallery is his work.

"Now, Martha, how did you make that wonderful game stew?"

A few days later Anna returned home from visiting her sister-in-law and could hear male voices in the parlour. Her mother asked her to take in more ale for the two gentlemen who had come to discuss business matters with her father. They rose to their feet as she entered. The older man was fair of complexion and the other taller man had a more weathered face. Even though his hair had been scraped back into a hat the older man was easily recognisable as a Danish sculptor she had seen at Chatsworth for his neatly trimmed little moustache and tiny beard just under his lower lip were distinctive but now his hair was spectacular being parted in the middle of his head and falling down in long chestnut coloured waves to his shoulders.

Her father introduced them:
"This is Caius Cibber and this is John Gardom. Please meet my daughter, Anna."

It was only when they spoke to her she thought she remembered the voice. Could it be the same man? The day the pony bolted on the way back from Calton she had been flustered and dishevelled but she had been captivated by his laughter. Now he was clean, his hair tied back in a ponytail, quite a tall man with broad shoulders. His eyes were widely set in his face. His mouth was wide and generous. He looked like a person one could trust. She could hardly utter her response "pleased to meet you both." Before she could rush away from the room her father explained to her that Caius was looking for lead to make garden sculptures in London. He had contacted the local blacksmith, John Gardom, who in turn had brought the Dane to their home; perhaps they could make a deal for the supply of lead. The gentlemen declined more ale, Caius saying that his work for the Duke was finished and he was returning to London as soon as possible. John Gardom said he needed to return home to Baslow, just down the road, but would very much like to come another day.

Oh yes, Anna really hoped that he would come again. She hoped he wasn't married. How could she be sure of seeing him? She would find an excuse to visit his forge in Edensor.

Everyone knew the Gardoms. They had been in Baslow for generations, farming, quarrying the escarpment beyond Far End and blacksmithing. Josh Greensmith knew John's father well, Thomas Gardom, a widower. These big strong men had a reputation of being hard working and had some standing in the community. It was obvious for all to see that John Gardom and his daughter, Anna were strongly attracted to one another. Although there was a few years age difference Josh told his wife that he approved of the match and hoped the couple would marry. As far as he was concerned, nothing should be put in their way.

Perhaps there was another Gardom son suitable for daughter Kate.

# CHAPTER THREE

**Baslow, 6th October, 1695**

We are nearly there. It is my wedding day. I can see the Church tower and its spire. John and my parents thought we should wait no longer and although the circumstances are difficult, in that not only will I have a new husband to care for but his all-male family too! However, I have decided to accept the situation. I am glad of the fine autumn weather. The old horse drawn carriage has been spruced up and decorated with foliage and accommodates my parents, my sister Kate and me. My dress, which has been lent by a Lady at Chatsworth House who had it brought over from Holland, takes up a lot of space and is very heavy. It was not a good fit for her, but with a few nips and tucks it does more than well enough for me. A few gold threads are interwoven in the deep rose coloured silk. The full skirt has a robed overskirt which is draped towards the back. Although I am slim the stomacher holds me in even more and there is fine pleating at the back of the bodice and on the lace trimmed sleeves. All these draperies are fastened with buttons and loops. My head dress is also borrowed; a small cap with stiffened lace decorations, not too elaborate as it would not be fitting for my station. The shoes did not fit; no-one will notice my bare feet underneath this extraordinary dress.

Mother, Kate and I have been very busy for the past few days in what is to be my marital home. I am to live with my husband at Woodhouse in the hamlet of Far End along with his father, Thomas Gardom and John's brothers Thomas and Christopher at their family farm. Mrs Gardom died a few years ago. My mother has told me that my life will not be easy, but with careful planning and good management she is sure that I can run a successful household. She advises me to get permanent help from one or two of the women living in the nearby hamlet as it is a big half-timbered hall house, mostly two storeys high if you don't include the attic rooms. A large central room with a big inglenook fireplace has several rooms leading off and the kitchens, having no rooms above, have high ceilings. The three chimneys are built of stone and the fires are always kept going. At present there are no permanent women of the household, although a rather rotund local woman, Mrs Howard, helps with looking after John's youngest brother, six years old Christopher, does some cooking and cleaning (not much by the look of it). John's father has vacated his large bedroom for us and we have a new four poster bed which has been made and carved by a local craftsman and then assembled in the room. My small oak chest with few belongings has been put in place. We have scrubbed and cleaned everywhere, carefully bleached with lime to whiten the elm floor boards upstairs and the oak stairs and the flagstone floors have been scraped of layers of accumulated dirt. The large heavy table and the benches remain in the big hall but the men have moved out much of the smaller pieces of furniture, except for the long cased clock, to make way for the wedding breakfast which is to be held at Woodhouse rather than at my parents' smaller home. Bunches of sweetly smelling lavender give a feminine touch, probably unseen in the old family home for a long time.

We have arrived at St Ann's Church. I just catch site of my brother Edward with his wife and children, scurrying into Church to get ahead of us; not quite late. Suddenly I have butterflies in my stomach. My mother and sister go ahead. "I pray all goes well with thee, lass" says my father and I calm myself then clutch his arm before we enter the Church. There are gasps and sighs from the women, probably at the sight of my borrowed dress! I think I recognise a few relatives and friends but I have my eyes firmly fixed on my husband- to- be with his brother William waiting for me at the end of the nave.

At the party later on I meet John's brother William for the first time. He is twenty two and resembles John but is not quite so tall. He is married to a farmer's daughter in Whitwell where they live and all is going well for him. But that wasn't always the case as he lost both his first 'wife' and child two or three years ago. My father-in-law and my parents have had a jolly time, imbibed and eaten well. Little Christopher has enjoyed all the attention from the ladies past their child bearing years. My other new brother-in-law, Thomas is eighteen, the same age as me, still living at home. How will I manage him? He is dark haired, quite handsome, but does not have the wide happy smile or the stature of my John. Where is my sister, Kate? It occurs to me that for the recent few days that we have been readying the house she has been unusually quiet; I did not notice at the time in my own excitement and the activity. She comes back into the room with more ale for Thomas and I can see her bright, sparkling eyes; it dawns on me that she has fallen for him in a big way! I am uneasy about it but cast my thoughts aside. Guests are leaving; I must join John to say farewell and thanks to everyone. It has been an amazing day; beyond my wildest dreams.

A few days later I notice that someone has carved a little heart in the oak panelling of our bedroom.

The first few months of marital status in my new home were really ones of discovery. Dorothy Howard still came in everyday to clean; with three hearths there was always plenty of dust. I enjoyed the cooking; Mother had taught me well and we dined royally off our own meat, eggs and produce. Little Christopher, with a mass of blonde curly hair, was a joy to me and so eager to show me everything; it was if he was discovering his home, animals, fields and woodland for the first time. If time and weather permitted we would go off in the afternoons to explore. He liked to paddle in the brook which ran close to our house. The steep sides had been edged with square blocks of quarried gritstone, not only so that we could step down and fill buckets with water, but also to prevent flooding of our land. The unpolluted water always looked clean and sparkling and was safe to drink avoiding the necessity to drink ale.

John, his father and brother Thomas worked all the daylight hours and I didn't see much of them until they returned home at the end of each day, tired, dirty and hungry. As the winter nights drew in they spent more time closer to home and my father-in-law set about repairing the old house and the farmyard buildings. In stature father-in-law resembled an older version of John. He had a high forehead and bushy eyebrows which overhung his sad grey eyes, a good strong, straight nose and wide mouth. I never heard him utter a rough word. He was perfectly natural with everyone, his courtesy was always the same, not just put on for visitors. I respected him. Sometimes he liked to talk about the state of the country and the news he had heard.

He was a mine of information that was gleaned when he traded with the millstone buyers and even more when he went to Haddon Hall and Chatsworth House to arrange for supply of stone and lead for building projects and repairs, where the nobility had first hand knowledge of national events. And of course, the staff overheard everything! Although I probably didn't realise at the time this was a chance to improve my education and young Christopher's.

I encouraged the family to sit a while after our evening meals and talk. On the first of these occasions Father-in-law began by telling us that he was born in 1636 when Charles the First was on the throne and who reigned without Parliament for a few years. Everyone still talked about his demands for ship money when many landowners had sold land and assets to meet these demands. And then of course, there was civil war in England; my own grandfather had told me that Rowland Eyre up at nearby Hassop Hall had turned his home into a Royal garrison. It was the scene of several skirmishes before the Parliamentary victory. Father-in-law and his older brother, Johannes (who went on to Cambridge University), had attended the charity school in Baslow and were very well aware of the brutal, bloody combat of the war nearby and they knew that the big barn at Hassop was used as barracks for the Civil War Royalists. When a troop of Royalist cavalry passed through Baslow on their way to the Battle of Naseby it caused a great deal of excitement. Oliver Cromwell was the Puritan leader of the Parliamentary side. It was a time of vast upheaval. Following the execution by beheading of Charles I in 1649 England became a republic under Cromwell. To his credit he established religious tolerance, but for a time there was no crowned Monarch. It was a time of revolutionary turbulence.

"Is there any more rabbit in the pot, Anna?" interrupted brother-in-law Thomas. I had made the mistake of not clearing away the plates before we got talking. Having cooked three rabbits my intention was to have enough for the following day; well I would just have to add more potatoes and carrots and they could have bread to mop up the delicious gravy.

"Now what was I saying?" Father-in-law continued with his dialogue. "Oh yes, it was a time of change by force." He told us that the main battles were at Dunbar, where Cromwell defeated the Scots, and at Worcester. The uncrowned Charles II had tried to claim the throne but after he was defeated at Worcester he fled to France. Cromwell was a highly influential figure and then began his appointment as Protector in 1653.

"Papa, what is a protector?" "A ruler, son" Thomas told the interested child.

Three or four years later a new House of Lords had formed and in that year Cromwell was offered, but declined, the Crown. When he died in 1658 his son Richard became Protector but resigned the following year, in fact, it was thought that the army made him abdicate. After the collapse of Cromwell's Commonwealth, Parliament accepted that the monarchy should be restored and General Monk brought Charles II back to England whereupon he was crowned King. Father-in-law thought that much credit was due to Parliamentary Government during the two reigns, rather than the Sovereign controlling politics but he still favoured the principle of a hereditary monarch. There was a leaning towards the Episcopal Church not Roman Catholicism and, furthermore, father-in-law and his friends did not trust foreign influence. The general population approved of the Monarchy, the Church and Parliament which gave rise to an enthusiastic welcome to Charles II. However, this rapidly cooled when he attempted to free himself from Parliamentary control!

All this type of discussion was completely new to me and I realised that family life with my parents had really confined me to local knowledge (and gossip), with sometimes a little information about the monarchy and as far as foreign matters were concerned that had been quite beyond my comprehension.

"Oh my goodness, Christopher, you ought to be in bed" I said rising from the table. "But I want to hear more" he retorted.

"Very well" said his father "we will continue another day" and giving me a wink said "come on, lad, I'll take you up; dare say you can get away with a quick wash of your face and hands for once!"

As they went up the stairs, to my relief, I heard father-in-law explaining that the Episcopal Church was one ruled by Bishops (I hadn't been quite sure about that).

The following evening, Christopher was fully washed and ready for bed before supper so that he could stay up and listen to his father.

"Is that all there is, Anna? Are we to go hungry?" Was my husband complaining? "Well, you shouldn't have eaten so much yesterday!" Of course I was laughing. "There is some good cheese, a bit crumbly, but fine flavour and there is extra bread and you can eat as many of our own apples as you like" I replied.

The three men had started talking about the plague, carried by fleas. I heard one of them say that wherever a flea jumped up, so did the plague. There had been several outbreaks during the past two or three hundred years. London had been rejoicing when James I was crowned but this was cut short by an outbreak. Then later when Charles I was crowned there was another destructive outbreak, but never as vicious as the London plague in 1665 when it was thought that over 100,000 people had died. Father-in-law was about thirty years of age when that happened.

This was followed by the terrible disastrous great fire of London. The catastrophic fire ravaged for five days and destroyed the whole of the inner city, but left the slum areas on the outskirts relatively untouched. There was new grand building in the city centre but the slums - or liberties as they were called - that had been fire damaged were replaced in much the same old way. Of course, the program of new building in the inner city meant that there was a great demand for building materials better than timber and thatch. Quarrymen, such as the Gardoms, had great demands made on them for their stone, which of course created more wealth.

I remembered that the previous evening we had been learning about Charles II.

"What happened to him – did he have his head cut off like his father?" asked Christopher.

"No, nothing like that, he had been a strong and fit man but became ill and died when he was aged fifty five. Everyone thought he would live much longer." Father-in-law answered the boy and then continued with his narrative by telling us that on the death of Charles II, the accession of his brother, James II, was undisputed. However, the new King quickly revealed that he wanted complete equality, both civil and religious, for his fellow Roman Catholics. He removed dignitaries of their roles if they would not accept Roman Catholicism. He created hostility in the Church and Universities. He tried to undermine the independence of local government; many Lords Lieutenant refused to supply lists of Papists and Dissenters who might be suitable for election to Parliament. In June, 1688 the trial of the seven Bishops of the Church of England came to court. They had defied a controversial order of the King and were accused of seditious libel – a grave offence that constituted rebellion against the Crown. However, they were acquitted, and that very day, William of Orange was invited to bring over an army to secure the liberties of the English people.

"Father, do slow down a bit" interrupted Thomas.

"Papa, papa, who was this orange man?" queried Christopher.

"This orange man, as you put it, is our present King who came to the throne a year before you were born, Christopher. He was a sovereign Prince, a Dutch man, of The House of Orange, a kingdom in the Holy Roman Empire."

"But papa, why did we want him?"

Father-in-law went on to tell us "It appeared that there was no legitimate heir to the English throne to replace James II. William of Orange's mother, Mary, was the daughter of our own Charles I – you remember, Christopher, the King who had his head chopped off. Her one brother was Charles II who had died too soon and her other brother is King James II, but who has caused so much trouble. Added to that, William's wife, Mary, is his cousin, the daughter of James II. Furthermore, William is a Protestant."

"So you mean to say that William was invited here to usurp his father-in-law" said John. "That must have required much sole searching – not something to be done lightly."

Father-in-law continued "It should be said that William had earned himself a reputation for making peace in Europe as he had resisted the French invasion, forced Louis XIV to make peace and concentrated on building up an alliance against France. Well, William promptly accepted the invitation to come to England, issued a Declaration listing the illegal acts of James II, and promising to abide by the decision of Parliament. William embarked for England. James escaped to France – abdicated."

"That was probably just as well really, don't you think? I don't suppose he wanted a battle with his father-in-law!" John had interrupted but his father continued.

"The throne was vacant but there was even greater confusion than the months which preceded the Restoration or those prior to the Civil War. Then there had been too many claiming legal authority; now there was no legal authority at all. People feared to carry out their daily lives because travellers were searched upon the roads by no warrant save the pretence of public safety; villages were held by mounted men, why, even our own Earl, who had up to now been obscure at Chatsworth, formed his tenantry into a mounted regiment. Town gates were guarded by the military, and all this solely in the name of the Protestant religion. The gentry and middle classes were up in arms, not knowing what to expect, whilst mobs were raiding Catholic chapels and mansions. The great English army, which had been legally disbanded by James as his last act, stood in confused and angry regiments distrusted by civilians. A smaller force of Irish Catholics were drifting about in search of safety, terror struck but also creating terror by rumours that they were on the march. English men in the grip of panic were drawn out from their homes as if for war, armed and excited and ready to use their swords against one another.

"What a terrible time to be living in" I ventured.

"Yes" said father-in-law. "You were probably too young to realize it, but we were once again on the brink of civil war and all Cromwell's efforts would have been wasted. The only place of order and sensible purpose outside this drifting chaos was in and around London where growing numbers of supporters of William of Orange were to be found. William arrived unopposed at Torbay in England on 5th November, 1688. But he could not, and did not wish to issue commands outside his own camp. A hasty Parliament was assembled in London the following month and unanimously voted the civil and military administration into the hands of the Prince of Orange. If the Parliament had hesitated, England, no doubt about it, would have been in flames by 1689. After much wrangling the Crown was offered and accepted by William with his wife Mary."

On that occasion our evening was ended by John saying to his little brother:

"And now young man time for bed. I'm sure Anna will explain it all tomorrow!"

***

My husband, John, was not often present at what I called his father's history lessons, as he was often away engaged in his beautiful wrought iron work at fine houses in Derbyshire and Yorkshire.

Although I had plenty to occupy me, I did miss my sister Kate and some intelligent female company. My parents were in good health; they did not need to keep her at home to look after them, nor indeed to work and so she was able to visit me at Woodhouse and stay several days at a time. Being quite a shy girl the men took advantage of her nature and teased her unmercifully, especially brother-in-law, Thomas.

One day in the spring my father, Josh Greensmith came to visit father-in-law and they took Christopher and me up to the quarry which was approached by a path through the wood at the back of the house and then a long steep walk up to the top of the edge. Before my marriage my father had told me that because of quarrying and mining the Gardoms had wealth. For as long as anyone could remember they quarried in and on the escarpment behind Woodhouse where I now lived. They made millstones, troughs, and gateposts in thousands.

Not only did they quarry the gritstone, but elsewhere quarried limestone and near where my father had workings. Limestone contains rich deposits of minerals and deposits of lead ore (galena). The lead mining was making my father rich too, but it was hard and dangerous work. Usually the lead was found by following veins in surface outcroppings, particularly in rakes or vertical fissures but now that all this visible ore had been tapped my father and brother were looking for other surface sources. Father-in-law suggested they might like to look further on from where his own men were working. We delayed for a short while to look at the breathtaking views from the top and where we could look down on our farm below. Father-in-law took the opportunity to speak with his men chiselling away at the millstones and further on we saw where they were hefting great blocks of stone for building projects. When we reached the desired area further on, knowing lead to be poisonous they checked for signs in plants and trees and any poorly performing crops. I gathered that they would then make soil probes and if these indicated favourable signs they would dig holes and trenches in promising places. The plan was to sink many shafts to a depth of up to 90 feet and then make underground galleries at which levels they could extract the galena. I could not envisage climbing down into the dark, dank unknown. Unfortunately, the site did not reveal any worthwhile possibilities.

When the winter days lengthened and Christopher and I could no longer explore our surroundings I set about teaching him some of the things that I knew. He was rather a slow learner but such an affectionate child, not too old to sit on my lap whilst I told him stories or gave him little cuddles at bedtime. My sister and I had been fortunate enough to attend the petty school in the village where we had learnt to read and write. I intended to ask my father-in-law if his young son should attend there after Christmas, weather permitting. It was obvious that he loved animals but his older brothers said that he should have knowledge of other matters. I hoped I would be able to take him to Chatsworth House one day and show him the beautiful paintings that I had seen there before I was married. And when John came back from working at the grand houses and mansions he told us of the beautiful artefacts, paintings and carvings mostly done by talented artisans from France, Italy and Holland who had come over at the time William of Orange had arrived in England.

# CHAPTER FOUR

**Woodhouse, 6th October, 1696**

The pain is unbearable. I have never known anything like it. It comes over me in waves; I cannot stop it. I want to scream. I want my mother. I think I will pass out. I want my mother, not any old woman from the village. Sister Kate is in the bedroom with me and I know she is distressed. Christopher has been sent as fast as he can go on his tough little pony to fetch Mother from Pilsley to tell her the baby is on its way. How long will this go on? More and more pain coming quickly now but then I automatically know what to do. When the contractions come - push down. The pain eventually becomes intermingled with joy as I know the baby is well on its way. Delirious, and now, real joy, elation… I hear my baby cry. I am exhausted and someone lays this little pink bundle on my belly to suckle. And then I sleep.

John is in our room. "We have a little daughter, our first wedding anniversary to the day; what a wonderful gift, but more so because you are both well. Your mother is here to take care of everything, so rest and do not worry. Kate will stay on a little longer to help."

A few days later another little carved heart appeared in the oak panelling of our bedroom.

We named her Elizabeth and she was christened in the Church of our marriage, St Anne's in Baslow. I thought I had been busy before but now I had this demanding little person seeking my attention all the time. Thankfully, although he wasn't doing very well and hated his lessons, Christopher was attending school. When he came home, of course, he now had to share my attention with his little niece. One day he came home with his father who had taken him up to the quarry as a distraction.

"Do the lad good to think of something else" father-in-law, had said.

There had been an accident the day before; one of the quarrymen got in the way as millstones were being rolled down the track into the valley below.

"Nasty business. Crushed his ankle. Don't think he'll be back at work. Probably lose his leg."

Father-in-law thought he should go up and calm the men, give them encouragement to carry on. Young Christopher was full of it and he couldn't tell me fast enough about what was happening up there on Gardom's Edge. That was the first time I had heard it called Gardom's Edge. He was shocked to see children even younger than himself labouring away. In the long term the visit may have done him more harm than good. He wasn't too anxious to go up there again and certainly did not want to follow in his ancestors' footsteps! No matter. Gardom's Edge was a major site for quarrying the gritstone and, to a lesser degree, in the limestone for deposits of lead. Originally it would have been done when farming was slack but Gardoms had been at Far End for generations and there were enough skilled men in the family to carry out all trades successfully. Christopher could eventually do something else.

So I had a new routine with my baby Elizabeth, Christopher sometimes at school, father-in–law and brother-in-law, who I now called Tom, out working long days and my husband, John, often working away. I missed him in my bed but when he came home he certainly made up for it!

***

The incessant driving rain beat against the leaded window panes until I thought they would break. More than once water from the yard had seeped under the back kitchen door until father-in-law finally channelled it away from the house. The resulting great floods in Derbyshire of 1698 meant that John could not get home for the birth of our second child, another little girl. Kate was staying at the time and delivered the baby which came so quickly neither of us had time to panic. John and I named this daughter, Catherine, after my sister.

***

My father and brother had still been trying to find new sources of lead; their recent exploits had not been very worthwhile. Eventually they found an area which looked very promising and I was told about the project based on the set up at another site in the Peaks.

"Steady on lass, don't think you should have come out so soon after giving birth" my father said as he held my arm to steady me. I felt quite dizzy looking down the shaft.

"But coming with you was a good excuse to get some fresh air now the weather has improved and the baby is well looked after by Kate" I replied knowing full well he was pleased to see me. "Besides, Christopher should know all about this."

Quarrying and mining, was giving our family a good living and my father was more than pleased to explain all the procedures involved. We were standing inside the miners' hut which was a lime stone walled cabin where the miners stored their tools, extra clothes and food.

"Are you going down lad?" Father asked Christopher.

"It doesn't look safe" I said looking at the precarious shaft. "Can't we just wait until they bring a load of ore up?"

So Christopher had no choice, but we didn't have to wait long. When the underground galleries were roughly constructed the workers climbed up and down the shafts, the entrances of which were usually within the miners' huts. The noise of the winding shaft outside the hut signalled to us that a load of ore was being brought to the surface. I was glad to leave the confined space and get back outside where we could see bigger equipment including baskets and sledges for carrying and windlasses for lifting. There was a flurry of activity as the men steadied and then tipped the load on to the ground. "Watch out!" someone shouted as we quickly moved away. How the miners, in what must have been a very dark, airless, wet underground tunnel, had managed to cut out and load the ore I will never know.

"Can we watch it?" Christopher was asking. My father, known to everyone as Josh, had told him that sometimes when the rock was very hard, to avoid heavy lifting they would resort to fire-setting. After mining had finished for the day a fire was made against the rock face.

"Oh no, lad, it's not at all safe and anyway we leave it to burn all night." He further explained that next day the back breaking job of fragmentation of the rock was made easier by throwing water on to it. The smoke from fire-setting, being deadly, meant this was a skilled technique and, therefore, not done very often. The poisonous lead dust could result in death or illness. Injury or death could also result from underground floods, falling rock or methane gas in shale workings and lack of oxygen underground in the badly ventilated galleries, and then when he and others in lead mining started using gunpowder that was yet another hazard.

"What happens next?" queried Christopher. Josh continued by saying that although malleable and soft, lead is very heavy and needs smelting into ingots for transporting in a manageable form. Sometimes the miner sells the ore on for lead extraction. The ore is then roughly washed of any loose minerals and dirt, riddled then smelted, usually elsewhere. Sometimes the dressing or rough washing of the ore can be done underground as this means less haulage to the surface and is particularly useful when there's a scarcity of surface water but an abundance at depth. One of the grime faced men had left the gang of workers and was coming towards us saying:

"What is Mrs Gardom doing here? This is no place for a lady and is this young master Christopher? Have you come to see where the work is done in these parts - we could do with an extra pair of hands." It was my brother Edward; I told him I was trying to show John's young brother how my family earned a living.

"I'll leave you to it then, we are very busy and there's a lot of lead to be extracted from down there; should keep us busy for quite a while."

"Where had we got to? Oh yes" said Josh "surface dressing floors are the most common and usually sited by the shaft top. The traditional smelter is a bole - you must have seen them - a large wood fire built on a hill and relying on two continuous days wind power (plenty of it in this part of Derbyshire). Often foot bellows are used to keep the hearth burning and some lead mines have water-wheels in a smelting mill. As you can see here, it all results in many piles of waste as the process only works with large pieces of rich ore."

Although we were not far from home I was anxious to return to my two little daughters and Kate. We said goodbye to Father and on our pony ride home I explained to Christopher that lead mining is a lucrative industry and many thousands of people are employed in the lead mines leading to great wealth for the land owners (the Crown usually), the mine owners, and the nation as a whole. It is exported to foreign countries and is second in importance to sheep for their fleeces and nearly everyone I know has sheep. As we journeyed the ground was so sodden in places that our ponies' hooves left great holes in a trail behind us. Whilst we stabled and unsaddled the steaming animals Christopher said

"I like being with my pony best....and you, Anna. I'll rub them down."

Since the great fire of London in 1666 there has been much new building and lead has been used on roofs of public buildings and the new houses being built all over the country by the nobility and gentry. All types of houses, including farmhouses, cottages and our hall house can have glazed windows with lead glazing bars. It is the only material for water storage and piping. It is also used for ammunition.

I hoped the new site would continue to be successful for my father and brother.

***

The stench was unbelievable and I quickly covered my nose and mouth with my shawl. As my eyes became accustomed to the light in the appalling hovel I saw him lying on the floor, lying on a dirty ragged blanket partially covering a straw pallet. The smell was emanating from what remained of his leg and he surely did not have long to live. I put down the basket of food which was immediately pounced on by a little swarm of dirty, pock faced children barely clothed in rags. They had come out from the shadows like vermin and then the woman appeared wailing and wringing her hands "What am I going to do missus?" I grabbed the already empty basket, rushed outside and was promptly very sick. "I'll come back with more" I shouted to the woman as I quickly found my pony and rode back down the Chesterfield road to home. It was a shocking experience and I decided it best to keep the whole thing a secret, at least for the time being, but would do my best to help the wretched woman when I could get away unnoticed. I made a couple more journeys to the hovel tucked into the hillside taking with me as much food as I could carry and a couple of blankets. My last journey revealed that they were no longer there, the injured man had clearly died and I later learnt that his wife and children had moved on to live with her sister, probably in another hovel.

# CHAPTER FIVE

## 1699 – 1701, More work at Chatsworth

John was very busy with ornamental blacksmithing and completing many contracts. I was so very pleased when he said he would be working from home now as he was needed back at Chatsworth House. We were in the year of 1699 and the Duke was starting to rebuild the west front and also planning to make alterations to the north front. John had met Jean Tijou again; they had worked together in the past and before I came on the scene. John wanted to bring the French master home so that they could look at the book of patterns for the creation of a new staircase. The foreigner came to visit at our home and I understood that he was a master blacksmith who would only have working for him someone who could work iron to perfection and with art! His appearance was quite scary and he stank of garlic, but he didn't seem to care. His mass of unruly hair was tied back in a colourful bandana and he sported a huge, unkempt beard. It was difficult to see any sign of a face behind all the overgrowth! His son-in-law, Louis Laguerre, married to Eleanor, had drawn a crayon portrait of Jean which was in the frontispiece of the pattern book; I'm not sure that it was a good likeness. The man was devoted to his flamboyant artistic ironwork, didn't speak much and what he did say was somewhat unintelligible to my ear. Probably a Huguenot, he had arrived in England in 1689 as a refugee because, being a Protestant, he had been forced to leave his country with many of his fellow craftsmen owing to the revocation of the Edict of Nantes in 1685. The French Henry IV had granted religious freedom to the Huguenots in 1598 but now that had been revoked by Louis XIV.

Life went on much the same for me but I made comfortable little improvements to the house and I loved to find fresh greenery and flowers from the hedgerows. Christopher had become a useful member of the household, 'though still hated school; he much preferred to be outside with the sheep and other stock. Being a hefted flock the Gritstones don't need too much shepherding. They are hornless hill sheep used to rugged country and they have attractive mottled black and white faces. At lambing time they are brought into the stone walled yard. The ewes are generally good milky mothers that have lively lambs and are able to get going quickly after birth. I hated their dirt and smell and kept away if I could. However, I did love the chance to go to market in Bakewell. Dorothy Howard would say to me "You go off lass and have a nice day out; make a change for you. I will look after the baby girls." And I knew that she would and I knew that she wouldn't do anything else but play with them all day! In the autumn, if the sheep had done well, there would be fat lambs to sell at the farmers market and I liked to go with one of the men of the family so that I could buy commodities, converse with the stall holders and other customers and see the sights; just generally have a good day out. The collies herded the sheep down the lanes to Bakewell and we would follow in the farm cart. I could see that the finished lambs were lively, well-proportioned and of good conformation and hopefully would fetch a good price. From our home at Woodhouse I loved to see the smoking chimneys of the Baslow houses below us as we descended the hill, to see the autumn colours of the trees as the leaves took on shades of orange, bronze and gold, and then we crossed on the bridge over the river Darwin, sometime the mist still lingering over the water making visibility poor and after a while over the next bridge across the Wye. The half-timbered thatched cottages crowded alongside the narrow streets in the town and near to the market square people had set up their stalls selling their wares. We were pretty well self-sufficient in the way of food stuffs but I could buy candles, baskets, earthenware pots, brass and copper items, cloth for clothes and blankets and all manner of things. Perhaps I would buy pretty bonnets for my two little girls or leather shoes for myself from the cordwainer. There were invariably working boots for the men that needed repairing. Sometimes I would see my mother and she could content herself that the Gardoms were looking after me properly!

Father-in-law still worked hard running the various family business interests and Tom remained living at home. It was comforting having my husband at home more often, though he, like his father and brother worked long hours. Time permitting, our conversations at the supper table, were not only about our immediate family concerns, or day to day work matters; if father-in-law could steer matters in his direction we would talk about "the state of the country" - his favourite topic! More often than not it was the Monarchy and the fact that we had a foreign King, William of Orange, whose intentions might be well meaning but who was not really loved by the people. And it was now well known that The Earl had been created The Duke of Devonshire for his part in bringing William to the English Throne. The Duke must have been more than peeved that the King had not made a visit to Chatsworth.

In January of the year 1700 our first son, Christopherus, was born. Luckily for me it was another easy birth but he was a small baby, did not feed very well and I worried constantly about him. I did not have any say in the matter when he was given the family name of his great grandfather. But it was easy to call him Chris. Sister Kate came to stay again. She had such pretty dresses and was wearing her fair hair in a very fetching manner – coiled up on her head with little stray curls at the nape of her long slender neck. She still seemed to be infatuated with Tom. I told her she was wasting her time; it was now very obvious that he had no serious intentions towards her, never had, though he still flirted with her: cruel man. John was involved in the creation of the west staircase at Chatsworth and there were also a lot of alterations and new building work which, of course, meant that there were still interesting characters about the place. I suggested we might invite one or two guests, especially whilst Kate was staying with us. She was such an attractive girl and I could not bear to think of her not meeting someone worthwhile. On one occasion, just Samuel Watson was with us and once more father-in-law brought up the subject of our foreign Monarch.

"Throw another log on the fire whilst your up from the table, will you Tom" said father-in-law. It was no longer a crime to discuss such matters as royalty or politics. I had always wondered why The Earl had played a part in bringing William and Mary to England and eventually asked if anyone knew.

"I will relate what I have heard, though in the strictest confidence, you understand." His big brown eyes carefully studied each one of us around the table before Sam lowered his voice. "Apparently, about four or five years ago, the Earl was banished from the court of James II for brawling in the palace at Whitehall with an old enemy of his, one Colonel Colepeper. Angry words passed and Colepeper struck the Earl, who retaliated and promptly knocked him down. For this the Earl was fined the outrageous sum of £30,000 by James's obedient and unquestioning judges. His mother, the Dowager Countess offered her son bonds for £60,000 which Charles I had borrowed during the Civil Wars. This was refused and the Earl fled here to Chatsworth. When the officers of the law arrived to arrest him he took them prisoners! Nevertheless, he had to give a bond pledging that he himself would pay the fine. In time, after James II took flight from England and William was on the throne, the written agreement was found and destroyed. That's why The Earl, as he was then, but now our Duke of Devonshire, favoured the Prince of Orange!"

We were to have visits from more of the artisans working at Chatsworth House and Sam nearly always brought them along to act as interpreter, for after all, he was working every day alongside these talented people. Furthermore, he was just as welcome in my home as that of my parents.

I think a little while after our son Chris was born, Sam bravely brought along a most articulate French artist, Louis Cheron, who looked tired with bags under his eyes. His soft face was framed by beautiful black curls, his lips were almost voluptuous and his nose was daintily tipped at the end; he could easily have passed for a woman. Father-in-law behaved in his usual charming manner, but I could tell he wasn't too keen on having the French man in our home. John bringing Tijou here was different, because it meant more business! Cheron was from a Parisian family of artists and trained under his father at the Royal Academy of Painting and Sculpture. He had won prizes in Rome and whilst there studied the work of Raphael and Giulio Romano. He returned to France, gained several commissions but in the wake of the persecutions after the edict of Nantes's revocation in 1685, like Jean Tijou, had decided to leave.

Meeting such interesting characters greatly enriched life for us and, indeed, for the whole area around Chatsworth. It was a period of enlightenment and learning, an insight into different cultures and lifestyles, not usually experienced outside London.

# CHAPTER SIX

## The years 1702 – 1706, Woodhouse

Queen Anne, at the age of thirty seven, came to the throne in the year of 1702. Her parents were James II and Anne Hyde and her elder sister, Mary, who died in 1694, had been the wife of our now deceased monarch, William. Both Anne and Mary had received a Protestant upbringing, although their father converted to Catholicism and remarried.

King William, had probably been misunderstood by much of his population, hated by some and he had made it quite plain that he found English Statesmen generally corrupt and intent on furthering their own gains. He could not find one friend or supporter, but by the time he died we thought he wasn't such a bad old thing! The English population as a whole didn't understand much about foreign matters, but because, as a family, we had regular contacts with the talented artists and craftsmen working at Chatsworth House, we were becoming rather well informed and Sam was able to convey to us his knowledge and understanding of events. Occasionally, we would be brought a very 'second hand' London newspaper. I already knew that William had invaded England in 1688 and then been offered the Crown by the parliamentary opposition to James II and eventually had became joint sovereign with his wife Mary.

I now learnt that before he came to England from his native Flanders he was made chief magistrate in order to resist the French invasion. He forced Louis XIV to make peace in 1678 and then concentrated on building up a European alliance against France. As my father-in-law had correctly told us, he had married his cousin Mary -- daughter of James II. He was invited by both our Whig and Tory leaders to take the Crown from James.

The Whig Party had emerged during the reign of Charles II when the Earl of Shaftesbury and his followers in the Green Ribbon Club attempted to exclude Charles's Catholic brother, later James II, from the succession. As a result, they became associated with the cause of the Dissenters who wished to defend the liberties of subject and Parliament against the threat of an absolute monarch. The term 'Whig' from 'whiggamore' or cattle drover, began as a term of abuse by their opponents. Although led by the nobility, the Whigs appealed to the interests of commerce and the professions. On the other side the Tory Party emerged as staunch supporters of the Crown and the Church of England. 'Tory' was initially a derogatory nickname, meaning an Irish bandit.

When William landed with a force at Torbay in Devon we knew that James had fled to France. It was obvious that William had left the country he loved for one he disliked but his one aim was to get the weight of England against Louis XIV of France. But the Treasury was empty; the armed forces starved and ill disciplined, the administration in this country was chaotic. By all accounts he was a tolerant man but known to have said he found the Church "hydra-headed with factions" and hostile to Roman Catholics and Dissenters. He wanted to choose his counsellors from the best of all parliamentary parties but that was a failure. In due course, James returned from France and led an uprising in Ireland but after being defeated by William at the Battle of the Boyne he fled back to France. William spent much of his time campaigning and after Ireland, in Flanders.

It was generally felt at the time that William's dealings in Scotland, his policies in England and his military campaigning in Ireland appeared to have been muddled but his successful campaign efforts with France in frustrating their endeavours to dominate Europe, if not the world, were finally appreciated. When James II was dying in 1701, still in exile in France, Louis XIV foolishly acknowledged the uncrowned James Edward (son of James II) as King. This action of attempting to weaken the European Alliance of England, Sweden and Holland against France was unwelcome and gave William a popularity he had not previously enjoyed. We English subjects at last understood that our civil liberties, which we now enjoyed, were not to be taken for granted and had been strenuously fought for by, our now deceased Monarch, King William III.

***

In the February of that year (1702) I was delivered of a son, Johannes. He was a tough little chap and suckled voraciously. He did everything sooner than my previous babies, but perhaps I was just comparing him with Chris. It was a busy household -still all the men living at home - but I now had extra help in the form of Mrs Howard's daughter, Jess, who was a great help with the children and lived in. I had my four children under the age of six, John's thirteen years old brother, Christopher, and three grown men, being Father-in-law, brother-in-law Tom and husband John. Our six bedroomed house was bursting at the seams. I jokingly said to John that perhaps we should move to nearby Haddon Hall as I had heard that there was no longer anyone in residence. Perhaps life at Woodhouse was too familiar and comfortable, but in all reality, why would anyone leave, apart from Tom?

A few days later, father-in-law surprised me by saying: "I am going to Haddon Hall today to see about some repairs to the stonework. One of the chimneys has broken and its fireplace is damaged. Would you like to come with me?" I had the opportunity of a short outing to escape from all this domesticity! I didn't need any coaxing!

Oh, yes, at first sight I fell in love with that pretty house built of locally quarried stone; everybody does (to me it looked like a small castle). Of course, I had passed Haddon Hall on many occasions it being situated only a few miles away. It looks securely built on a rocky outcrop above the river Wye and seems to jut out from the hillside which is thickly covered with attractive trees. The picturesque house built on the slope, one quadrangle above the other is approached through the archway of the gatehouse with its massive doors of squared oak, along a pleasant drive and across the bridge over the river. Beyond, where the drive turns to ascend the slope up to the Hall, are the Elizabethan stables from which, father-in-law told me, an underground passage goes to the Hall. The south west front of the Hall with its stone balustraded terrace overhung with little pink roses and broad flight of steps up to the property, was something I had not seen before; I liked the informality of the planting which partially disguised the stonework. We didn't have a garden at Woodhouse, just a grassy area down to the stream. We rode round to the side, passing under the gateway in the north- west tower and I felt the full impact of the massive embattled walls towering above. Here we left the horse and cart and walked up the wide steps into the lower courtyard, which was surrounded by ranges of buildings that didn't quite seem to meet up owing to the slope of the land, and, watched by the grotesque gargoyles, we entered the castle. A caretaker took us through the cavernous kitchen which, having very small windows, was dark and had little ventilation. Apparently, the kitchen staff had worked by candlelight. We continued through passageways, which echoed with our footsteps, into the galleried banqueting hall with its massive fireplace and antlers around the walls. I noticed a strange contraption, which the caretaker said was a manacle and lock. It was for any guest 'who did not drink fair' and would have his hand manacled and the remainder of his drink poured down his sleeve! Charming! The great room was still furnished and I imagined wonderful parties had been held there. The long narrow sturdily legged table was placed on a dais a few inches above the level of the stone floor. The caretaker said there were much finer tables upstairs. At the other end of the hall, placed nearest to the kitchen, was a carving table, with a circular groove cut into its surface to catch the gravy. There were big carved oak and walnut chairs - I particularly liked the high backed ones having caned backs and turned legs - long benches, court cupboards and I glimpsed fabulous tapestries, but nothing as rich as at Chatsworth House. I preferred it; less ornate and much more tasteful to my mind.

On that occasion it wasn't necessary for father-in-law to go upstairs and so I didn't see the bedrooms and galleries. It was obvious that one would need an army of staff to run such a place, but it seemed a pity that the owners had gone to live at Belvoir. However, they wanted the property properly maintained and father-in-law said I could accompany him again if I wished.

Being indigenous to the area, I had always known the history of the place and was pleased to tell Christopher when he asked about my visit.

William the Conqueror's illegitimate son, Peverel, and his descendents had held Haddon for over 100 years before it passed on to the Vernon family and then in the sixteenth century, through marriage, to the Manners family.

Christopher asked if he could accompany his father next time he went. I didn't enter Haddon Hall again for a long time. I did not mind. From then onwards, Christopher spent more time with his father. He was no longer at school and he hadn't been bright enough to go on to the Grammar School, in fact he had hardly mastered reading and writing. It was best for him to learn a trade by his father's side.

My visit to Haddon prompted a desire to have a garden, or at least attempt to grow a few flowering shrubs. A herb garden would be a very good idea. Mother had given me a copy of Lytes Herbal of common herbs, a complete physic whereby a man may preserve his body in health or cure himself with such things that only grow in England, they being most fit for English bodies. Another well-known herbalist, Culpeper, believed that nature had provided in every plant the antidote to a particular disorder, if only the connection could be discovered. I knew I should replace the lavender and rosemary which had gone woody. I was amused when I read that rosemary was good for weakness of the brain and for fidelity! Lavender has many uses. Comfrey would be a good idea as it makes a good poultice for bruises. I'd need a mortar and pestle. It would be easy enough to raid the vegetable garden for such things as onions and potatoes and perhaps plant some garlic. Hot potato water was used to ease the discomfort of rheumatism and onion was supposed to be a cure for gout. There was a plentiful supply of nettles in the hedgerows and I was already hanging bunches in the larder to keep away flies. We had a couple of old apple trees; an apple poultice was good for sore eyes with which the men were often afflicted after working in the smithy shops. I thought I would like to plant raspberry canes, for, apart from the delicious fruit, raspberry leaf tea was a useful daily tonic prior to childbirth. One of the men could dig me a little plot near to the kitchen so that I could try my hand at cultivation, time permitting. Well, I would make time, somehow. I wondered if I could keep bees, as honey was a natural healer which, according to my herbal, could draw out and cure infection. But then I thought it would be easier to barter for some with one of my neighbours.

***

I was too ill and shocked to be present at the burial of my little baby girl. Even the date is vague except I knew it to be in the year of 1705. It had been such an uncomfortable pregnancy; I carried her awkwardly and she was badly presented for birthing. Had I been a ewe the little unborn lamb would have been carefully turned so the head came first in the normal way. I drifted in and out of consciousness completely unaware of what was happening in my household or round about me. My recovery time seemed slow. My dear sister, Kate had moved in for a while and was taking care of everything. What a blessing. What a Saint.

One day I realized that there were now six little hearts carved in the panelling of our bedroom; one for our marriage and five for our children. I realised how blessed I was. Poor Queen Anne had been married for twenty two years to George, Prince of Denmark, and had lost so many babies. I think only one had survived for a short while - she must have been devastated.

John was kind and loving, but too loving, for to my horror I realized that I was expecting another baby. It dawned on me that as I had no baby to breast feed I had so quickly become pregnant again.

***

"Come on, Anna, we are all waiting for you. I have a surprise." John was calling me. "Wrap up warm. Come and see."

I clutched my nearly new sleepy little baby boy to me and cautiously went down stairs. I could not see the other children. "Where are our children, John?" I asked.

"Come on, Anna they are waiting outside."

What a surprise! I still could not see my children, but I did see a beautiful black carriage harnessed to two sturdy black ponies. I was speechless. John helped me into the carriage, where all my children, under thick blankets, were very quietly waiting. I felt quite overwhelmed.

"Is this borrowed?" I enquired of my laughing husband. He still had that lovely laugh which had captured my heart a few years ago.

"It belongs to us, bit better than a cart or trap, don't you think?" He said "I've done some repair work and made a few changes to make it comfortable. It is well made and strong so it's ideal for use on the bumpy roads round here. I needed to replace my old ponies; these two new ones will cope handsomely for work and pleasure. I thought that my family deserved a treat. You've not seen much of me and we can go on little outings. I thought we'd go up to Hassop Hall today so that you can see what I have been doing there."

I sat facing my four grinning children huddled together; although summer it was a chilly day. Elizabeth was now ten years old, already quite a young lady and sometimes bossy. Catherine was much quieter than her sister; a bit of a day-dreamer really and very fond of six years old Chris who loved his books. Four years old Johannes never seemed to look clean and tidy however hard I tried; today was no exception. Our baby boy seemed very contented in my arms. John climbed up front and away we went. (I learnt later that John had accepted the carriage in part payment of an unpaid debt). We went down the well-worn road into the village, past the Church and then past the watchman's hut close by the hump back bridge which took us over the river. Every able bodied man was expected to take his turn in watching the village through the hours of darkness until dawn and to turn back any undesirable characters who tried to enter the village. The cold dark hut wouldn't be an encouragement to fall asleep whilst on duty! Our journey took us along the leafy lane at the back of Bubnell and up to Hassop. After a while we passed through the heavy iron gates, which John proudly showed us as his work. The old half timbered house, three storeys high, dating back many, many years, stood tall on the hill. The Catholic Eyre family owners were staunch Jacobites, had lived through a testing time of persecution, and suffered a great deal during the reign of Elizabeth. After the Civil War when the house had been captured they had to pay handsomely to redeem it. I explained to my son, Chris, who had a voracious thirst for knowledge, that the Jacobites were Catholic Stuarts. With the death of the last Stuart King, Charles II, and the accession of the Protestant William of Orange in 1689, the loyalties of many Scottish Highlanders were directed to the exiled James II. But now was a time of peace. John and I, with our children, walked in the grounds and he showed us the wrought iron railings so delicately scrolled and the matching gates into the parkland. He was pleased with his work, and rightly so. It was hard to believe there had been such violence at Hassop; it now seemed so peaceful and the views were breathtaking.

On our way back "Let's just venture up Bubnell Lane and see what the new house looks like" said John.

Life wasn't so bad, after all. Christopher was seventeen and worked full time with his father and looking after the farm along with the two local men from the cottages in the hamlet where we lived. Brother-in-law, Tom was spending a lot of time at widow Broomhead's. She lived at the new house in Bubnell. Her husband, Robert, had died a few years ago in 1699 and they had no children. Their business interests were similar to the Gardoms' and she had asked father-in-law if anyone could help. Her brother-in-law, John Broomhead who lived further up Bubnell Lane did have children, but they seemed to be carving out their own careers.

I think my husband thought that there might be a chance of us moving to the new house. It wasn't that new, in fact, construction on it had started in about 1664, but it was one of the newest houses in the area at the time. I hardly dared to consider the possibility of living there; it seemed so grand, double fronted and well proportioned, built of stone and with a proper slate roof. I had counted many chimneys. There was obviously a huge reception hall upstairs with its beautiful stone mullioned windows where one could look out on the nearby river and across to St Anne's Church. I thought it was the loveliest house I had ever seen. We talked about it in bed that night.

"Do you really think we might be able to live there, John?" I had never expected valuable possessions, or a grand life style, but I knew he was doing well in his own right, employing many men and with blacksmiths shops at Edensor, Baslow and at home in Far End.

"We'll have to see, my love. Now let's get down to more immediate matters." His ardent love making had never diminished.

Eventually, I learnt that there was a John Broomhead who had been smelter to the Manners of Haddon. He very likely made much wealth for his employers, curried great favours with them, and the beautiful new house was built for him. At least, no one remembers anyone else living there before him. When he died his son, Robert, took up residence whilst his other son, John was further up the lane at another fine but older property, Bubnell Old Hall.

# CHAPTER SEVEN

**1707 – 1708**

"Anna, there is a young talented artist I have been working alongside. He is English and has completed his apprenticeship with the foreign masters. I would like you to see his work. It's a long time since you've been to Chatsworth House, why don't you come? The Duke has kindly given permission and you can bring the girls and your sister, Kate. You can manage the ponies and the carriage now if you take it steady." John was right. I hadn't been to the House for a long time. A little outing would be beneficial, especially to see the splendid house. Our daughters were old enough to behave properly and my sister was still unmarried. Maybe she would meet someone young, handsome and eligible!

He had a lovely soft accent and told us he was born in the West Country, in Dorset. For a young man of about thirty years, James Thornhill, had painted some amazing large scale murals. On the ceiling above the west stairs, where John had been working, was a painting entitled: "The Fall of Phaeton." This was one of his earliest efforts and it was a wonder Thornhill hadn't fallen off the scaffolding; I felt dizzy looking up at it. He enlightened us with the tale from classical mythology. Phaeton was the son of Phoebus (the Sun) who was allowed to drive his father's chariot for one day but lost control and plunged too close to the earth. He thereby caused part of the Turkish Ottoman Empire to be parched into barren sands and all Africa to be, more or less, damaged, the inhabitants blackened and vegetation nearly destroyed. He would have set the world on fire had not Zeus transfixed him with a thunderbolt. After reassuring the girls that it was only a story we continued our tour through the fabulous house by entering a lobby where the ceiling and all the walls seemed to be completely covered in paintings; they showed the abduction of the Sabine women by the Romans who were helping to populate the newly founded city of Rome. I did not think that an explanation was appropriate at this particular time and hoped to gloss over it should the matter arise too soon in the future. In the library were wonderful panels which Thornhill had assisted Louis Cheron with. Yes, Cheron had been a guest in our home. We were interested in the technique used for this wonderful work and it was so refreshing not needing an interpreter to translate from excitable long winded, gesticulating artisans! The method employed for creating the murals was by painting on to fresco secco; a dry lime plaster which had been strengthened with animal hair. Once dry, Thornhill's method was to float in lead oxide and when that was dry, paint directly onto it in oils.

Sam Watson was there too, eager to show us his latest carvings. Masses of oak panelling had been bought for the Great Chamber in the State Apartment. Our friend had carved out of the contrasting silver coloured lime wood all manner of things which were suitable for a banqueting room: fish, game birds, fruit and flowers. We had already seen his carvings in the chapel and his carvings of swags and flowers adorning the cantilevered Great Stairs, but now he showed us outside to the richly decorated courtyard where I couldn't help noticing a beautiful wrought iron balcony at first floor level (must be the work of John, I thought). Sam's work was so prolific and we admired his carvings of weaponry and armour. Suddenly aware that the sky above was looking somewhat overcast I dragged my girls and sister away hoping to reach home before we got drenched and promising to return as soon as possible to see more beautiful paintings and Sam's sculptural carvings.

***

"Come quickly, Mama." I could hear my son, Johannes shouting. He sounded alarmed. "Grandpa has fallen. I cannot manage to lift him."

"Don't fuss, lad, I'm just a bit winded, but I'm pleased to see your mother." The old man was quite shaken, but eventually, making sure no bones were broken, we got him into his chair by the fire. Having applied crab apple verjuice to his bruised knees and, thinking it might dull his senses a little, I gave him a glass of brandy from the small bottle which Louis Cheron had given me. I banished from my mind the thoughts of our Queen having a fondness for the spirit. The brandy was stored in oak barrels for transporting from France to England and was supposed to be refreshed with water prior to drinking. However, the English had discovered that if it was kept in the barrels for some time it changed and became more palatable and didn't need watering down. My intention had been to save it in a secret place for a special occasion! After that incident I watched my father-in-law quite closely and observed that he often walked into objects and that he no longer wanted to read. Sadly, I realized that his sight was failing and I worried about him falling down the stairs. There was only one solution; we could move his bed into the small parlour. Cooking was done in the adjoining kitchen and we would just have to make do with using the big hall for eating and everyday living, besides, it would free up a much needed bedroom. How I wished we could all move to widow Broomhead's house at Bubnell.

***

My growing family, for now I had another daughter, Ann, born in January of 1708, were all blossoming. Elizabeth and Catherine spent happy hours spinning and weaving and they cleverly involved their grandfather, who was now confined to the house and the immediate familiar surroundings.

Son, Chris, a spindly lad, liked his books and was a good scholar. Perhaps he would, one day, follow his great uncle to Cambridge. Father-in-law delighted in their many discourses. “Tell me what’s going on in the world now” he would ask and get his clever young grandson to read to him and then expand on his knowledge.

Without any doubt, Johannes, although only six years of age, was going to be the next generation blacksmith! He meddled with everything and he was always black!

And what of my baby boy? I hadn’t really wanted him; the pregnancy was too soon after losing my daughter, but he was such a happy, cuddly soul. Why hadn’t we got a name for him? I couldn’t continue calling him “baby boy!” Despite my protests he had been christened Thomas, but I could not have three men in the house with the same name; it was ridiculous. I took the opportunity, whilst we were all sat round the table after supper, and invited suggestions from my family. One of the children offered: “How about Sam, or Edward?” Elizabeth suggested George. “We haven’t got a George in the Family.” And that was it, settled: George Thomas Gardom - but only for a while. We soon lapsed into calling him Tommy, two names were too much, but I still thought of him as my baby boy because he was so cuddly.

It had always been father-in-law’s task to make the ale but now it had to be taken on by someone else in the family. Christopher was willing to be responsible for this vital part of our daily life; it was usually safe to drink the brook water, but the working men, especially in the blacksmith shops, needed plenty of liquid. When the subject was raised there were guffaws of laughter from my husband: "how will you get Father to part with his closely guarded recipe for his home brewed ale?" Well, I thought that Christopher and I would find out but I would not interfere, although in the end it did take me a long time to uncover the secrets of this mystery! Besides I was anxious to keep my menfolk away from the hostelry in Baslow as such establishments often had a reputation for bawdiness and wenching. Of course the home brewing took place in an outhouse, we called it the brewhouse, which was well equipped with a brass furnace and cauldron to heat the water, a brewing vat, a cooler, funnels, a collection of tubs and buckets and of course, barrels. I learnt that the best raw grain to use was barley – the grain not too fat nor too thin, not too dry and not too wet. The malting process, as it was called, was started by using the finest of water to wet the grain which was allowed to sprout, thus yielding sugar. Then the process was halted, the grains allowed to dry before being crushed or mashed with a hand mill or quern to release the flour and without damaging the husks too much. I heard father-in-law saying to Christopher "It must have no wefte nor tayle and not be drunk under five days old! It doth make a man fat and doth inflate the belly!" Whatever did it mean 'no wefte or tayle?' I gathered that it was important to get the ingredients in the right quantities because the ale was easily spoiled so it was a challenge next to add just the right amount of scalding water to the brew. Eventually, I went to investigate how Christopher was getting on. "Can you see your face in the liquid, Anna?" he asked. Apparently that was a sign that the liquid was cool enough and could be drawn off and kept until ready to be drunk after the stipulated time. Further, weaker brews could be made with the remaining mash, but I had frequently seen the mash being fed to the cattle, therefore there was no waste. The barrels of ale were kept in an outhouse where we also over wintered potatoes and other roots under straw and earth. I loved the smell of apples and pears in their wooden racks.

I think father-in-law was sad at having to pass over the ale making. The brewhouse had been his private domain where he could escape for a while if he needed to and he could often be heard talking away to himself. But really, despite his failing eyesight and increasing frailty nothing much passed his notice. "Do you know, Anna, there's a new type of ale in London now. They call it porter and it is made in a proper brewery house and only sold when the condition is right for immediate drinking. I should love to taste it and be able to make it." "Well," I replied "we shall have to get some for you next time one of our friends is coming back from the big city." We were in the kitchen together having a quiet little time. He was sat at the kitchen table and I was making oat cakes for him on the griddle which hangs over the fire. "I've got fresh butter and, just a minute, I will fetch from the back kitchen something special I have made for you." From the back kitchen beams sides of bacon and cured hams hung along with bunches of herbs and nettles to discourage flies. Bags of flour were stored on the shelves and there was an invaluable slate cold shelf always in use for helping to preserve the life of perishable foods that little bit longer. Every available beam and post had useful things hanging from them. We needed a lot of everything with always so many mouths to feed. "See what you think of this preserve made with plums and lots of sugar. It has set like jelly." Our big wide fireplace was furnished with all manner of ironwork: the essential heavy cast iron fat bellied cooking pot, with the evening's supper quietly cooking, hung over the fire on its ratcheted hanger dangling from an iron sway (sometimes I would let the three stubby legged pot rest in the heaped up ashes, but I didn't want it to cook too fast on this occasion), there was a big spit for roasting meat supported by tall iron fire dogs and turned by a pulley wheel on a weighted winch. When in use I would have a big iron dripping pan underneath. I had both iron and brass kettles and pans. "I remember, Anna, that at Haddon Hall years ago in the big kitchen they had a huge spit and it was turned by a dog wheel… Eeh lass, this really is lovely….. It was quite literally a small dog scampering around…..Is there any more?" I laughed and said "You won't want your supper. It's one of your favourites, a mutton stew."

The brewhouse had its own special use, but we also had a wash house with a very large copper container with a rounded base set into a brick plinth. The fireplace underneath was fuelled with bavins, or bundles of sticks and it had its own little chimney. We used it constantly, not only for washing clothes, but to heat water for all manner of reasons including a weekly bath night when pitchers of water would be carried in to fill the tin bath having been placed in front of the parlour or kitchen fire. In actual fact, the wash house was a better place to take a bath and I often did just that and in privacy. On other days we usually had to content ourselves with jugs of cold water and basins in our bedrooms. Unless the weather was fine enough to wash clothes and bed sheets in the stone sided brook ('though we hadn't done that for a long time) it was done in the wash house. Every Monday was wash day which started in the early hours as it took a long time to get the fire going well enough to heat such a large volume of water and then the whole room would be filled with steam. I was glad to have help with the laundry in the form of a local woman, Mrs Briggs, who could generally be left to get on with it without supervision from Dorothy Howard, though I often heard her saying "Now don't you get those coloureds mixed up with anything else." There was a definite routine to it all with four separate piles: white bedding which went into the copper first, dirty – usually very dirty - work clothes soaking in a large earthenware pan, coloured clothes and then underwear washed separately. The dirtiest clothes had to be scrubbed and dumped in a wooden barrel and a wooden dolly plunged up and down to loosen the dirt first before washing in clean water with soap made from grated animal fat. No wonder Mrs Briggs had such strong muscular arms and when it was all clean enough to her satisfaction she could be seen wringing out the clothes, her big capable hands red and rough and then she would peg out on to the wet-heavy hemp clothesline strung across the yard using the gipsy made split wooden pegs. In the summer the bed linen was often flung over the stone yard walls to dry and the sunlight seemed to whiten and make it smell nice. The dirty water from the copper was carefully transferred in a pitcher and hand emptied. We all knew to keep out of her way, for without warning, still with her sleeves rolled up, Mrs Briggs threw the water about; anyone in the way would get wet! Then with the big bass broom she scrubbed the wash house floor, the privy floor, the stone flagged yard and anywhere she could reach.

Next day, as regular as clockwork, Mrs Briggs would be back to tackle all the ironing. She heated the flat irons by the fire, testing with a splash of water till they hissed, and then ironed everything on top of a folded old sheet on the kitchen table, all the while singing out of tune. Dorothy Howard had once asked her not to keep up this monotonous chant, but the woman seemed so offended that I suggested to Dorothy that on Tuesdays she should clean the bedrooms and keep well out the way. I did not want any discord in my household and I could not manage without either of them.

# CHAPTER EIGHT

**9$^{th}$ November, 1709 Bubnell Hall**

We are walking up the wide oak staircase with its heavy turned balusters. Despite the dull day, with winter fast approaching, there is laughter and merriment. The banqueting room is beautiful with its huge stone mullioned windows, letting in the mottled light, even on this dull day. It is how I imagined it. There is a good fire in the big carved stone fireplace though I know it will soon be too warm with all these people. From the leaded paned window at the side of the room I can see the sparkling, fast flowing river and from the window at the front, where in places the trees do not interrupt the view, I can see the Church tower and spire and all the carriages and traps in the courtyard below me. The horses and ponies have hay bags, as if they are due for a lengthy stay. The bulbous legged oak table is heavily laden with every food imaginable; Widow Broomhead has gone to town for her niece, in no uncertain terms, especially as there is such a scarcity of food now. And I must say that my brother-in-law, Tom Gardom looks very handsome in his Sunday best. I am trying very hard to be happy for him and for his bride, Elizabeth. My sister Kate, although invited, is not here but for the moment I must put her to the back of my mind and I can no longer dream of living in this handsome house, they now call Bubnell Hall, as Tom and Elizabeth are to live here with Elizabeth's widowed Aunt Katherine.

"Never mind, Anna. It wasn't meant to be." John is at my side, he places a glass of wine into my hand; it is as if he has read my thoughts. I am not used to strong drink and it quickly goes to my head. I think that I must see what my children are doing, that's if I am capable. John is laughing "let's have a jolly good time and not worry about a thing." How sensible he is; I do love him.

Our daughters, Elizabeth and Catherine look so pretty and are holding the hands of their Uncle Christopher. The little children are running around. William and his family are here and, to my relief, are taking care of father-in-law; they haven't seen him for some time and must be shocked to see how his sight has failed. I meet lots of people; mostly they are just names I have heard during conversation round the table at home. Everyone looks beautifully dressed for the occasion and I too am pleased to be wearing a new fine woollen rose pink dress under an extravagant black velvet cape. John quickly gets into conversation with, I assume, work contacts and from time to time I hear his laughter. Christopher has now been introduced to some young ladies of his own age. Good.

Where are my daughters, and furthermore, my sons Chris, Johannes and Thomas? (Ann is at home with Jess). I am drawn to one end of the room where a little crowd has gathered. All the children, not just mine, are sat on the floor completely captivated by a young fair haired man who is entertaining them. He is very handsome and he is wearing the most beautiful frilled shirt with lace trimmed voluminous sleeves. His breeches are black, stockings white and on his feet the shoes have beautiful silver buckles. I can see his dark blue deep pocketed jacket thrown over a nearby chair. He speaks almost in a whisper, but the children hear his every word and watch his every movement. Ah, I see he is a conjuror or a man with a very adept sleight of hand. By his fine attire and his accent I get the impression he is not local. How clever and thoughtful of widow Broomhead to hire an entertainer to amuse the children. Someone tells me that he has been working in London and that he is very successful. Well, I suppose he is kept busy in the fashionable houses of the rich and famous.

Oh, I see that James Thornhill is here; I didn't know that he was back at Chatsworth. He is such a skilled artist. How polite of him; he is coming across the room to speak with me - we say hello and I am pleased to see him again.

"Have you eaten, yet, Anna?" he asks me. I tell him that I didn't think I was very hungry, but he is guiding me to the table.

"Look at that beautiful pyramid of apples and pears and oh, the oranges," I say to him "they have been carved out to make pretty patterns."

Mr Thornhill tells me that he has been in London and, although fashionable it is a disagreeable place to some, including the Monarch. The smoke from huge coal fires makes life intolerable, especially for invalids. He goes on to say that as I probably know our Queen suffers from gout, so can hardly walk. Life in general is tedious for her, and travel by carriage through the rough surfaced streets of the City exacerbates the debilitating pain in her joints. Despite the fact that she prefers to live in Windsor or Bath she has built an orangery at Kensington Palace. The white panelled interior has Corinthian columns and Grinling Gibbons has done exquisite woodcarvings. Outside there is a Portland stone terrace. William of Orange used to import plants and shrubs from around the world but they couldn't survive the English winters. "Have you seen this building?" I query. He affirms and I cannot resist asking if the carving is as good as Sam Watson's! He nods and then proffers "As you have brought the name of my dear friend into our conversation - I cannot see him here, by the way - I don't mind telling you that I am painting a portrait of the lovely gentleman. That is, Sam Watson, not Grinling Gibbons!"

"What else have you been doing recently?" I enquire and he tells me that he has a commission for the Worshipful Company of Drapers, to paint panels for a splendid carriage to be used in the Lord Mayor's Parade. He goes on to say "I don't know where they get some of their ideas, and I have had to do some intensive research. They want paintings of the Roman God Neptune and his companion spirit called Amphitrite. I do hope that what I have in mind will be acceptable." I think Mr Thornhill is too modest about his work as I think that he is very talented and I shall follow his progress with great interest.

"Let us see what else is here to tempt us. Pick up a fork, Anna, and a plate. Ah, one of my favourites, a magnificent battalia pie filled, I suspect, with little fishes and clarified butter. Do you prefer the game pie? It looks easier to cut. I think I'll miss the spit roasted pike; it can be rather bony and indelicate to eat. Shall I carve you some of that succulent pork ham; when I came to your house I remember eating from one that you had cured with black treacle and smoked over wild juniper wood. It was absolutely delicious." I let him continue as he was so enthusiastic and knowledgeable and I was enjoying his company. "And here is herb pudding, but I don't think I have room for it." I see that there are in fact two spectacular looking battalia pies which have been made in the usual way, each with a well dried pastry case formed to look like the round tower of a castle. The inside case will have been coated with egg and then, the one I know, and as James has already said, is filled with all manner of pieces of fish and topped up with drawn butter or some kind of savoury custard and then cooked in the oven. I know that one is fish for it has fish heads poking out of the battlements and I do not fancy it! The other one is probably filled with pieces of chicken, pigeon, rabbit, sweetbreads, other offal and even oysters which are not too difficult to get. I have already espied the cut laid tarts, and will save space for one after I have eaten some ham. Their fruit and creamy custard contents have been decorated with little pastry shapes. There are some moulded jellies and custards, which are now so fashionable. It is all quite delightful.

All too soon it is time to leave before it is too dark to see our way home. I find my husband and we prepare to say farewell and thanks to widow Broomhead, but she is talking with the entertainer. Politely, they turn to include us in their conversation. I am introduced to him but do not catch his name. He bows low, takes both my hands and at his touch I feel an exciting tingle shoot through my body. I pray no one realizes my embarrassment. We have to drag the children away; they have had such a wonderful time and I realize that so have I!

# CHAPTER NINE

### 1710, Father-in-law

Christopher found him. He was asleep in front of the fire. I came down stairs and looked in on father-in-law, as I always do, and saw that Christopher was kneeling on the floor, his head in his father's lap. I took in the scene for a few minutes and realized that Christopher was weeping quietly and then I knew. I crept away and went to tell John that his father had died in his sleep.

It was a bitterly cold day, the fifth of March. It was a bitterly cold winter. We left the children at home in the care of Jess and her mother Dorothy Howard. Despite the ice and snow, somehow those sure footed ponies got us safely to St Anne's Church - just John, Christopher and me. I hadn't known how the sexton would manage to dig the grave through the icy ground near to the church. The Reverend Joseph Nichols had conducted a very thoughtful and sympathetic service, which was well attended, considering the appalling weather. Our good friends William Barker and Edward Heathcote were there and, to my amazement, Thomas Peace our neighbour who had never been very friendly. (Perhaps we had upset him long ago in the past). He was with Ezra Cook who worked for us; another neighbour from our little hamlet. Tom, Elizabeth and widow Broomhead kindly welcomed us to Bubnell Hall for the wake, but, to my knowledge because of the bitterly cold weather, no-one stayed long.

***

We burnt the old bed and returned the room to its original use as the small parlour. I could not bear the thought of using the room as a bedroom again, but of course, it would still hold memories for all of us, whatever its use. John allowed me to buy a small gateleg table, on which my copper jug, a wedding present, took pride of place. I acquired some three legged stools which wouldn't wobble on the uneven floor and the girls wove and made brightly coloured cushions. Mrs Howard cleaned up the old pricket sticks and we put new candles in them. The precious hook and spike brass lantern clock was returned to its shelf on the wall. My brother had made and given to me, a brass chestnut roasting pan that I hung beside the fireplace. I rediscovered the brass candlesticks which had been packed away in a chest together with some pewter plates, a quantity of good table linen and all manner of things. The room looked refreshed and homely.

***

Thank goodness the weather was improving. I had picked some yellow winter jasmine, like golden jewels, and arranged it in the copper jug. When John came home he said that Sam Watson was coming to visit. He hadn't visited us for some time, probably due to the winter weather. I was listening out for his big heavy horse (Sam was a big man) and was confused to hear the "clip clop" of something lighter as well. Yes, it was Sam and to my amazement, riding alongside him on a smaller horse, my sister Kate. "Anna, John, we have something to tell you." Taking his time he tenderly lifted Kate down from her horse and I ushered them into the house so they could tell us their news in more detail.

"Your dear, lovely sister has agreed to be my wife!"

I was anxious not to show my disappointment. "Come into the little parlour and I will find something very special for us to drink." There was some cider brandy from the West Country, if I could lay my hands on it. I must say they both looked very happy. I did not think my sister would fall for such an older man, forgetting that my husband was thirteen years my senior.

"When will it be?" I asked and then Kate imparted without hesitation "In two weeks time at home at Pilsley Church and then we will be living at Heanor. We want you all to come to the wedding. Ma and Pa have given us their blessing."

There was little I could do or say. Naturally, I wanted my sister to be happy. Over the years we all had become very fond of Sam, but I thought of him as if he was an Uncle, not a suitable husband for my younger sister.

As they were leaving a little while later I heard Sam remark "By the way John, I hear that Jean Tijou has disappeared, left London, left the country. Don't know what it's about, but he didn't even say goodbye." John seemed surprised.

***

Their wedding was a very quiet affair, but nonetheless joyful, and afterwards Kate set up home with Sam in Heanor, near to Derby; sadly I knew I would not see very much of her now as our lives were changing. Sam gave up work and I understood that his health was not very good. I just hoped he had not married my sister for her to be a nursemaid to him.

***

Deciding to make the most of the early summer's day I had taken a couple of old blankets outside and we were spending an idle afternoon on the grassy patch near the babbling stream. In the meadow on the other side the mass of buttercups were like a shimmering golden carpet. It was a rare treat for me to day dream and for the children to play outside in the sunshine. Catherine was making daisy chains and Elizabeth and Jess were firmly holding the hands of Tommy as they paddled and splashed about with shrieks of delight in the shallow, cold water. Little Ann, who had worn herself out running around, was curled up by my side.

"Where does the water come from, Mama?" asked Catherine.

"I presume you mean the water in the stream" I replied.

"Yes, it always looks so clean and sparkling."

"Catherine, that is a very sensible question. It comes from a spring somewhere on Gardom's Edge and, as far as I know, it has never stopped running. It reminds me of the legend of St Anne and how our church got its name." At the mention of her name my daughter, Ann, stirred from her slumber. I waited until she was fully awake and then continued. "Many, many years ago there was a drought when all the ponds and lakes dried up, then the running streams and brooklets and eventually the springs and wells so that people were perishing for lack of water. It just so happened that there lived in a little village among the hills a very wise and beautiful girl whose name was Anne. People came to ask her what they could do. When she told them to cut deep into the rocks of the hillside where they would find water they were unbelieving and treated her with scorn. In the evening after they had departed, Anne used a stonemasons hammer and chisel and went among the big rocks and although some did see her go they would not follow but laughed at her even more. That night many people died from their terrible thirst, but when the sun arose in the morning, a stream, as clear as crystal just like this one here, flowed through the valley and the remaining people drank and lived. They followed the little stream to its source where it arose from a cleft in the rocks. A hammer and chisel lay there, but the lovely Anne was never seen again. Then they saw it was the work of a saint and dedicated the village church in Baslow to the girl."

"Oh, what a lovely story" said Catherine, but before she could say anything else we were interrupted by her noisy brothers.

"Off with his head" shouted Chris. The boys were playing soldiers with plantain stalks and striking one another's soldiers until one or the other's 'head' fell off. "I don't want to play this anymore" wailed Johannes. "I want to play the other game. It's more fun." "Well, I'd rather read my book" said Chris but then, obviously thinking better of it they were making guns by looping the stem of the plantain around itself just under the head, and then, holding the loop tight in one hand, sharply pulling the stem with the other hand so the head shot off, just like a bullet. These games were gentler than their usual sword fighting with sticks but how did little boys know about such things as fighting and war? It was no longer necessary for them to learn the use of bows and arrows but it was not long since the Muster Roll, an ancient rule that Baslow had to provide a certain number of soldiers and sailors for the King's service. The men were chosen by their fellow townsmen and they had no option in the matter. Furthermore, every boy in the village should have had possession of a bow and two arrows and practised with them every day. John's grandfather, Christophera, had been on the

Muster Roll of 1638. I secretly suspected that the Gardoms had come from strong fighting stock.

My normal daily efforts were concentrated on running a happy home and, to the best of my ability, educating my children. Elizabeth and Catherine worked hard at home with their spinning and weaving; Elizabeth, now fifteen, was talking of turning her skills into a business and both the girls could sew beautifully. The cushions they had made for me were very pretty and well stitched. Naturally, I was teaching them to cook. Chris was attending the grammar school and Johannes the little petty school in the village. Jess took charge of Tommy, my cuddly boy, and little Ann; they just played and squabbled all day like normal healthy children. Mrs Howard still came every day and brought us all the local gossip! Christopher seemed happy looking after the livestock and sometimes went to help his brother Thomas at Bubnell, or wherever they were working. I had suggested to John that it might be a good idea if his young brother went to stay with William at Whitwell for a while. It was a big farm and I knew they would be glad of an extra pair of hands. Besides, it was a large village and, hopefully, he would meet some young people of his own age. It was easy to get one of our men to do extra hours and look after the stock for us. And so it was; they always needed extra wages.

"Mama, can we have the magic man?" Tommy's little voice interrupted my thoughts. "What was that you asked?" I opened my eyes, rolled on to my side and looked at my son. "Please can we have the magic man for my birthday? You know, the one who was at the wedding" he asked again. I wondered which one of the older children had put the idea into his head. "Well" I replied "I don't really know much about him and I don't think he could come all the way from London and at such short notice" hoping that my reply would end the conversation, although, of course, I didn't want to disappoint the little chap. It was doubtful that we could run to such an expensive treat. Besides, the sudden thought of him had sent a quiver through the very core of my body; it was a risk I could not take.

"We know who he is" chorused Catherine and Elizabeth. "His name is Richard. Papa knows him. We have heard him talk about him." I had the strange feeling I had been set up for something - surely not - not by my own children. The desire to cool off in the stream by sitting on the stone blocks and dangling my feet in the cold water was a great temptation, but with great strength of mind I resisted.

"Well now, shall we get the rest of the ham and that nice crusty bread we baked this morning and have our food out here on the grass. Let's make the most of this beautiful day." I needed to distract them from such an idiotic notion. An entertainer, of all things!

***

He had only been gone a few days and we all missed him terribly. Elizabeth and Catherine hardly spoke. I hoped that I had done the right thing; it was my fervent hope that Christopher was settling into life at Whitwell and that he would be happy.

"Mama, if we can't have the magic man can Christopher come back?" I don't know who said that.

Little Tommy was four years old and the only one of our children to have a summer birthday. It would be a good idea to have a party; cheer us all up, so on the nearest Sunday I invited my brother, his wife Elizabeth and their brood to come to us after worship. Perhaps my parents would come too, though they were getting a little frail now. Chaotic it would be, but never mind. The girls could help me to lay on a feast! All being well all the cousins could run around outside for a while.

***

The smell of freshly baking bread had brought John into the kitchen. We had an oven at the side of the fire and bundles of wood (faggots) were burnt fiercely inside it with the door firmly closed. When the wood was completely burnt up it was hot enough to start baking; the ashes of course were scraped out before the dough was slipped into the oven on a long handled paddle. "Smells lovely, as usual; makes me feel hungry. Hope there's no bits of charcoal stuck to the bottom of the loaf" remarked my husband. I suddenly thought of my mother who didn't have an oven so she used a pot turned upside down in the hot ashes and baked in that.

Ignoring his remark about the charcoal I grasped the opportunity to talk to John about the disappearance of his former master, Jean Tijou. "Won't his absence in London leave an opportunity for some other master craftsman?" I asked. "Does he have a successor?"

His reply surprised me "I have considered it, but I cannot go to the Capital, even if I wanted to. I have work in my own right to complete at Castle Howard. There will be plenty of blacksmiths ready to go and make the most of the obvious opportunities in London and make their fortunes. One of my colleagues has already mentioned it to me, but I will be sorry to see him return to the City as he has been so useful to me since he arrived in Baslow."

“Well John, I am mightily relieved to hear that you will not be going to London. So will you be staying at Castle Howard for long?”

“Until the job is done, and if there is more, I will take it on.” It was unlike him to be so abrupt. “Would it please you if Christopher returned whilst I am gone? I don’t like leaving you without a man in the house.”

Without doubt, I knew that all my children would be pleased about that.

# CHAPTER TEN

## 1711, Richard Oddy

Happily for me John managed to get back from the North Riding for the christening of our daughter, Maria, on 7th June, 1711. She was the sweetest little baby with big blue eyes and a little rosebud mouth. I begged him to stay longer but he insisted on getting back the next day. He looked tired, his voice was sometimes scratchy and I noticed a slight hesitation in his movements; at least this had previously escaped my attention. Where was his infectious laughter? I realized with a shock that he was probably getting too old at forty seven for the hard work that he was undertaking. He promised he would soon be finished at Castle Howard but complained about the amateurish plans and instructions he had been given and his work had not gone as well as he had hoped. Although the main building work had more or less been completed two or three years ago there had still been iron work loggias, ornamental tunnels and gates to be done for the grounds as well as chairs and small tables for the terraces. They were being crafted at the Baslow workshop and were to be taken up at a later date by two of his men. Unlike Chatsworth House, it was a completely new mansion built for Charles, the third Earl of Carlisle. He was a member of the famous Kit-Cat club, a group of wealthy characters who were at the centre of London's social life, but like many people, had decided to return to their country estates or find a healthier place to live. John said he would draw a sketch for me, but its most dramatic feature was the round dome which seemed to crown the building.

His departure was unsettling. It seemed such a long distance, a rough journey, but the weather was pleasant, and he had ample provisions and warm clothing for the journey. Hopefully, I would persuade him not to go away again. No sooner had we seen John off on his journey, than Christopher arrived from Whitwell. They must have passed one another on the road. The children threw themselves at him, hardly giving him chance to dismount. My joy at welcoming him back was quickly dashed when I saw how thin and pale he looked. When he eventually broke free from his nieces and nephews he put his arms round me and choking back the tears muttered "Please don't send me away again." He was such a softy.

In John's absence he was head of the household and Christopher quickly settled back in. Between us we devised a plan so that he could always stay at Woodhouse and, whereby, he could make a living and I hoped that John wouldn't mind. I knew he wasn't interested in quarrying; besides Tom Gardom was overseeing that. John had a competent manager in Edward Heathcote, employees and associates working at the blacksmithing from his three workshops so there didn't seem to be any opportunities there either. John also had productive parcels of land in other places including meadows near Edensor. However, there were many, many acres of land under Gardom's Edge, much of it rough ground and woodland. If we got more pigs to turn over the rough areas and forage in the woods, the woodland could then be coppiced to stimulate growth and produce better timber and if we increased the sheep flock we could improve the grazing and make the land more productive. I hoped that his experience helping his brother, William, at their big farm would stand him in good stead. But first of all it looked as if he needed to get his appetite back and get a rosy glow back on his cheeks. That was easily solved with some good food. Perhaps one day I would discover what had made him so unhappy, but for now I thought that the time spent away would, more by luck than judgement, eventually have a happier outcome for him.

Apart from my nagging thoughts and concerns about John, we were getting back to being a happy household again.

***

Catherine had asked me about the Kit-Cat Club. I was explaining about the group of young men with literary and strong political associations who were committed to the promotion of Whig objectives. They would meet at the Trumpet Tavern in London and at Water Oakley in the Berkshire countryside. However, the first meetings were held at a tavern in Shire Lane run by an innkeeper called Christopher Catling. He gave his name to the mutton pies he made, known as "Kit-Cats" from which the name of the club is derived. Upon hearing the explanation there were hoots of laughter from my children and who afterwards were frequently heard to refer to their brother, Chris, as Kit-Cat. And, yes, I promised to make them mutton pie later in the year.

A messenger arrived with a letter from Sam. Kate had given birth to a little boy but, sadly, he had died after a few days. My mother had now gone to stay with them. I felt so useless; there was absolutely nothing that I could do to help or comfort them. My sister had been a tower of strength to me on so many occasions. I returned a letter to say that perhaps Sam could bring her to stay for few days before the nights drew in.

Sam had also sent me a newspaper, so thoughtful of him. I missed the discourses of days gone by between my father-in-law, Sam and occasionally, John. It would be good to read the 'news' even if I had received it a few days late. And I think much of it was not to be believed. It was meant to be witty, the few words referring to the Monarch:

'Sarah Churchill manages the Queen, Marlborough manages the war and Godolphin manages the Parliament.'

Sidney Godolphin of course, who came from an ancient Cornish family, had served both Charles II and James II and for the first few years of her reign he was Queen Anne's closest political adviser. But my life was so busy I had little time to think of Sarah Churchill, her husband the Duke of Marlborough and their relationship with royalty, or of politics, or of wars that didn't really affect me or of the financial state of the country. For the time being there was little outside Woodhouse that could concern me.

***

When John did return a few weeks later he was not alone. The delivery, by two of his men, of fancy iron terrace furniture completed the Castle Howard contract. But they had found their employer unfit to travel back by horseback and, making sure he was well wrapped up and reasonably comfortable, bundled him into the empty work cart for the long bumpy ride back home. We got him into the house as quickly as possible. His breathing was coming in short gasps and he complained of pains in his chest. My immediate thought after seating him in the wainscot chair was to burn some dried nettle leaves on the parlour fire – we always kept a fire going because it was too much trouble to try and start again with a cold hearth – and if he could inhale the fumes they would help clear his bronchial tubes. Not knowing what was wrong with my husband I didn't risk giving him brandy, but the home brewed ale went down well with him and his parched anxious men. After a while, and seeing John improving, they left for their own homes in Baslow.

It was patently clear that John could no longer work away from home, if, indeed he could do much work at all. I wanted to keep him at home; nurse him until he was well again. Keeping the house quiet with all our children was going to be difficult, but would have to be done and the older ones would have to take on extra chores to free up my time for their father. There was still plenty of blacksmithing and ornamental iron work to be done, for under the training of Jean Tijou, John had earned himself a prestigious reputation. Although he seemed to be improving since his return from the North Riding, he was no longer such a fit man and decided to ask one of his previous colleagues for assistance.

I always remembered the day vividly that Richard Oddy entered, not only my home, but my life, although I didn't realize that fact at the time. My confusion at seeing the man was of total shock and disbelief. There must have been a mistake or I was dreaming.

"Hello, Mrs Gardom. It is pure delight for me to see you again, and may I say that you are looking more beautiful than ever." He bowed low and took both my hands, as before. I quickly removed my tingling hands from his grasp.

"You are Richard Oddy?" I stuttered. "I was expecting one of John's colleagues, not a gentleman such as yourself. You are the entertainer from London, are you not? You were at Bubnell Hall at the wedding party two or three years ago. My children have never forgotten you." (Neither had I).

"Mrs Gardom, I'm so sorry if I disappoint you. I am a gatesmith, somewhat like your husband, but I have been working in London for too long. Whilst there I have picked up a few tricks for entertaining children and it was easy for me to acquire a gentleman's clothing in order to play the part. As I dress now is how I usually look."

We both began to laugh, something I hadn't done for some time. We were in the big hall and slowly, as if by magic, except for the babies, all my children appeared, tip toeing in, one by one, and sat on the floor in a circle around us as if they were expecting a performance. They were so quiet. This man certainly had a magical aura in more ways than one.

"Mr Oddy, I think you have come to see my husband, shall we not delay?"

"I'll be back soon" he whispered to the children. "Be good for your mama."

For a financial consideration it was arranged that Mr Oddy would take over some of John's work. Apparently his specialty was not the ornamental blacksmithing that John and his men produced, but less ornate and with output more prolific and less time consuming. Not everyone wanted flamboyantly styled gates and garden railings. He was happy to leave the big city and take lodgings in Baslow. Naturally, he needed to return to see John at Woodhouse about various projects on several occasions. I tried hard to retain my equilibrium when he visited. Occasionally he would stay a little longer and share our supper. Life in London was a fascination to me and everyone I had met who had worked in the big city and then come to Chatsworth seemed to be successful. It was strange for me as a country woman living in the wilds of Derbyshire and yet being able to meet and sometimes mix with such talented people. It was definitely an example of two worlds that were poles apart.

Richard's success in London had developed because of his work for John Sheffield, 1st Duke of Buckingham, a favourite of Queen Anne, who in 1705, had decided to build himself a fine house on a site which had been in private ownership for some 150 years. Apparently, during the reign of James I a plantation of mulberry trees for the rearing of silkworms was established in the garden, but it transpired the wrong variety of mulberries had been planted which were unsuitable for silkworms! But to continue with John Sheffield, finding the existing house very dated in appearance, he demolished the building to create the new Buckingham House. From there Richard (we had dispensed with formalities and had easily adopted the use of Christian names) was engaged in many more contracts for ironwork for the nobility and the rich for their grand houses and who always desired something better than their neighbours – at a price.

The forge fumes were obviously detrimental for John and really it was better for him to stay away, or at least, only inspect the completed craftwork. Sometimes John's health rallied and on good days he would take the pony and trap to visit the smithies working for him. Johannes liked to accompany him and we agreed that if the boy was so interested he might as well start learning about the skill of hitting black iron as soon as possible. Prompted by John I told Johannes as much as I could about the history of blacksmithing.

Thousands of years ago it was discovered that some types of rock would yield a substance (iron) when exposed to high heat and then become solid when cooled. From this substance simple tools and eventually spear and arrow heads could be made which were sharper than stone. Later it was discovered how to make charcoal which burned at much higher temperatures than an ordinary wood fire and then the men could find and extract much better quality iron. The earliest method of producing iron was in a small furnace built of clay.

“It was called a bloomery.” said John trying not to cough.

The fuel used was charcoal and was made to burn hotter with the use of hand bellows. Small pieces of the rock, or iron ore as we call it, were placed in with the charcoal and after several hours a small piece of iron, called a bloom, was produced. This could then be hammered into the desired shapes for tools and weapons.

“We blacksmiths suddenly became very important and as the production of iron increased more uses were found for it; this also meant that new skills to work with it were learned and developed. There weren’t really any further developments until the thirteenth century when the bloomeries were able to increase in size by means of water-wheel powered bellows like the present Gardom forge where the stream had been damned to do exactly that.” John so badly wanted to impart his knowledge to his son but he started coughing until he was almost breathless. I suggested we paused for a while and fetched him some linctus, afterwhich I continued the narrative.

Blacksmiths became more specialized and were more in demand to produce weapons, armoury, tools and then they branched out into chain makers, nail makers, swordsmiths, armourers and so on. The next step was the introduction of the blast furnace and large quantities of cast iron were produced, but it had different uses. We could see the delighted look on our son's face as he realized how his father's work had such an interesting history and that wrought iron had developed over the years, and of course he had seen how it could be teased into such beautifully shaped objects. I told Johannes that the role of the blacksmith was very diverse because not only was he a man who could make or contrive articles, he was sometimes called on to act as dentist, doctor, undertaker, animal doctor and horse dealer. He was a man who would hold an important position in the community, such as magistrate or Church warden. Years ago what went on in the darkness of the smithy was a mystery to most people. Many people thought the blacksmith was a magician or even a witch, indeed, many stories evolved about the 'man of fire.' Perhaps that was the origin of stories of the Devil in burning hell. Plainly people generally didn't understand that the smithy was the master of his iron work with the ability to understand the properties of the iron that he could alter by heating, beating and hardening; it was not a mystery or magical to him.

Very often the blacksmith's shop was a meeting place where all the local gossip was exchanged and many business deals were made. Johannes learnt that a blacksmith, not only shoes horses, makes iron tyres and repairs wheels and farm machinery, but also makes many kinds of useful tools and other objects by heating the iron in a forge to make it soft and then hammering it on an anvil to shape it. If he was to follow in his father's footsteps as an ornamental blacksmith, an artisan, he would learn the art of wrought iron to create beautiful gates, balconies, pagodas and even, perhaps, furniture. There would be no end of possibilities for him and John's talent would live on through him.

***

"You got the old shoe, Gulley?" Johannes and I were at the blacksmith shop in Baslow run for us by Edward Heathcote. Gulliemus Chapman, local tinker and traveller, was there - dressed in his grubby smock and baggy old trousers tied with bits of string below the knees – there with his huge gentle horse waiting to be shod. "Ah good, that'll save me making a new one. Now you just keep hold of him; he's a big animal." We stood outside with Edward as he lifted up the back leg and the horse leant a little towards him; I could see it was an enormous weight and bending over must be back breaking work. Edward rasped and trimmed a little off the hoof, tried the shoe for size and then handed it to the boy to heat in the forge. Now supporting the foot on a tripod to take some of the weight there was fierce hissing as Edward pressed the red hot shoe into the horn of the horse's hoof and we smelt the burning horn. The horse did not flinch "Most horses are well behaved but you get the odd one that isn't" Edward told us "but now I must be careful to drive the nails in at the right place and not ruin him for life by driving one in at the wrong angle."

"So, master Gardom, I understand that you want to be a blacksmith and farrier like me and your father" Edward addressed Johannes who nodded. "I see you have brought some chain to be repaired, just let me finish off here with Gulley and you can watch me perform a few simple tasks. See what you think of it all. Don't suppose your father has had chance to show you much."

Once inside the shop the heat from the forge was almost overwhelming and the glare of the fire lit up the faces of the smithy, us and his boy helper working the long handled bellows. Because the blacksmith understands the strength of iron and knows how to regulate the hardness he can make his own tools for cutting, shaping and punching when the object he is repairing or making is cold, or more often than not, when it is hot. He needs such a variety of tools for the different jobs and the long handled ones used for hot work are kept separately from those used for cold work; the tools used for hot work if mistakenly used on cold iron would be easily blunted. When wanting to cut iron the blacksmith grasps a chisel and strikes it with a sledge hammer. Sometimes for a bigger job the chisel with handles is used and the assistant wields an almighty blow with the big sledge hammer. We could see rows of tools used for shaping such as swages, fullers and flatters. As a farrier he needs the special tools for shoeing such as rasps and paring knives that we had seen him take from the tool tray laid out before him when he was working on the big horse. Behind the tray of tools we could see on an elm block a swage block with a multitude of recesses and holes used to guide hot iron into shape. The array of tongs all round the forge were made by Edward Heathcote himself and were for grasping every size and shape of hot iron. We could see that he had been in the process of making decorative wrought iron scrolls for more gates in the park at Chatsworth as they were all precisely shaped and lined up on a work bench – no doubt this was work he could do between farrier work and repairing broken farm machinery.

"Right then, young man, I think you want some more chains made and I have some wrought iron bar here which will do the job. This involves some welding so don't get too close; I am protected by my big leather apron. The two ends of wrought iron are brought to white hot so that sparks begin to fly from the iron, then we hammer the two ends together fast and furiously." He proceeded to the anvil near the forge and the loud hammering sounds were ringing out loud and clear. "If you fail to get both ends to welding heat they will not unite; if you make them too hot they will simply burn away. Now, see - what do you think of that?" As almost an afterthought he said to Johannes "Has anyone explained how we make wrought iron?" Johannes shook his head. Edward looked across to me and mouthed tut tut! "This is the beginning of all wisdom; we need to know the difference between wrought and cast iron. Now, if I hit a piece of cast iron with a hammer it will smash because it is brittle and won't stand shocks. On the other hand, if I hit a nail it will bend because that is how wrought iron behaves. It is altogether more useful than cast iron and it is the stuff that we blacksmiths want."

"I know about bloomeries and blast furnaces" said Johannes. "Good" continued Edward. "The iron from the bloomeries is a kind of wrought iron but you can't make very much of it and there is an awful amount of slag. The job of the bloomery is to free the iron from the iron ore which is best described as a mixture of rust and clay.

Bloomeries are not really hot enough so the extracted lump has to be hammered to make the slag squeeze out and the iron sticks together until eventually most of the slag is squeezed out and you end up with an iron bar, just like all the iron bars you can see here. Cast iron is made in a blast furnace, the bellows driven by a water-wheel so that the furnace gets hotter using charcoal as before. But now the iron is freed and the clay forms a greeny coloured slag with limestone which melts and runs down inside the furnace as does the melted iron, but the slag is lighter and floats on top of the iron. From time to time you can run off the iron, run it into moulds called pigs for remelting. Or you can cast things directly. So there we have it – two kinds of iron – wrought and cast. You can hammer and forge wrought iron but cast iron is brittle and breaks and you can only shape it by casting it so it's no good to blacksmiths. You can weld wrought iron but you can't do that with cast iron. Cast iron is too brittle to make chains – as you have just seen you need wrought iron for that. Cast is alright for cannons or hammer parts but its use is very limited to us."

"Can you make wrought iron out of cast iron?" queried Johannes. "Well" replied Edward "that's a very interesting question. I think it would be a very slow, messy process because you would need two furnaces and there would be a lot of hammering, but it would be useful because wrought iron is in such short supply. Young man, I shall give it some thought!"

He showed us some pretty cupboard door hinges to be repaired at a later time. There were pieces of iron of every size and shape which created a scene of muddle but he always seemed able to find that odd bit he needed for the job in hand.

"I've got a new wood chisel blade here, part of a set for Sam Watson so I'll just show you how to harden it by heating one end to red hot and then cooling it in this big tub of water – swishing it around a bit. The idea is to get a strong sharp end and then work gradually up the blade to a softer blunt end where it fits into the handle so that the blade doesn't snap when he's using it. When I temper it by heating the blunt end watch how the colours change and creep down the blade from light straw, to dark straw then blue and next brown and finally pale straw. Now that last colour is reached we'll quench it or cool it."

I decided my son had seen enough for today; what a lot he had seen and learnt and Edward had been such a delightful tutor.
"Oh, I almost forgot, Edward, we brought down a flagon of ale for you." I thought he had earned it!

Before we departed Edward asked if we could take back a repaired scythe for Ezra. He had sharpened the blade and repaired the handle with some new fittings to hold it in place. It seemed the variety and work of the smithy was never ending.

Johannes had enjoyed his time with Edward Heathcote and was eagerly waiting to get back home to tell his father all about it.

# CHAPTER ELEVEN

**3rd November, 1712**

Oh, unhappy day. They are here to witness the will. Normally I would have been so happy to see them: Richard and Roberta Johnson, Ezra and the Lawyer. John's breathing and coughing has been so severe that it has taken several hours for the scribe to record it all. I have been resting in a chair with my feet on a stool for most of the day for I am very heavily pregnant again. My belly is huge. Heaven knows, I could have done without this; it has to be my last pregnancy. Elizabeth and Catherine are looking after the visitors, and in fact, young as they are, are running the house. Mrs Howard, who has helped me all my married life, bustles about and mothers us all; bless her.

A few days later on November 15th, Richard Johnson is here again and together with Dorothy Howard, they witness a further condition to the will that John has written himself. I am not privy to the contents of either document being a mere woman.

At the end of November I am relieved, mentally and physically, of a son, William; another strapping baby with a good pair of lungs! Thank goodness for Jess; she just loves the babies. The nursery is her domain.

Word soon gets round that John's health is failing him. Friends begin to visit, a distressing time for all concerned as he has great difficulty breathing, let alone conversing. Despite the weather, James Thornhill brings Sam Watson to visit and we are very pleased to see them. Sam has a slight paralysis down one side of his face; must have suffered a little seizure, but otherwise seems alright and I am pleased to hear that my sister, Kate is in good health. James is as charming and considerate as ever and I can see by his expanding waist line that he still enjoys his food. Although distressed about his debilitating condition, John is clearly delighted to see them and I try to persuade them to stay a night as we could somehow make a bedroom available for them with the use of a truckle bed. I think Christopher would be quite amenable to giving up his room and be comfortable sleeping in the stable with his new brood mare! However, they take their leave and I am reassured that they are not travelling all the way back to Heanor, but breaking their journey with my parents at Pilsley before darkness falls.

***

Somehow we always struggle through the long, cold Derbyshire winters, but now with John being ill it is difficult to raise our spirits. The children are so quiet and each one of them must be so upset to see their father the way he is. But I try to see that they all have little projects to occupy them and that they attend school whenever possible, weather permitting. More than once I have been at my wits end not knowing what to do for the best for my sick husband. But the cough linctus made with rose hip and elderberry syrups is pleasant for John to take and, if nothing else, eases his throat when parched and rough. Thank goodness for the honey from Ezra's bees, which with warm water and cider-vinegar, helps to ease congestion. His breathing comes in short gasps. John can no longer climb the stairs and once more the little parlour reverts to a bedroom. Life is not easy and one day I realize, with a guilty conscience, that Dorothy Howard has lost a lot of weight and is looking tired. She is getting on in years and is probably saddened to see us in this plight. She has been with the family for many years and will probably die on her feet, working for us. That's the way it is.

***

“It’s my turn to stir the pudding.” Little Tommy was getting anxious as he thought he had been left out. It was ‘stir-up Sunday’ and we were making the plum pudding for Christmas. All the children were taking it in turns to have a stir and dipping their fingers in to taste the alcoholic fruity mix and I had added a few lucky silver coins which always caused excitement.

“Don’t forget to wish” says Catherine.

“And what will you wish for my beautiful daughter – some handsome young man to sweep you off your feet?” I say, and she blushes.

One day John had said to me, between bouts of coughing: “Let’s celebrate Christmas and give the children something they will never forget.” The thought of Christmas had passed through my mind several times but I hadn’t known how to approach it. Would it be a quiet or a joyous occasion? John must have sensed my apprehension. He continued: “Get Dorothy Howard and her husband to join us. I doubt if they have anywhere else to go and I know old George likes a drink or two. He’s particularly partial to the spiced ale we always have and it’s not as if they have far to go home. Jess always likes to be here with the children. Elizabeth and Catherine will help you with the cooking – I have already asked them. My brother, Tom, will come up beforehand and bring little presents for the children.” So it seemed that it was all arranged! All I had to do was decide whether we would have goose or turkey. I knew that Christopher was fattening both. We could have both! We enjoyed fresh meat and poultry in the cold weather; at other times of the year it was only sensible to eat preserved salted meat.

The mood in the house was immediately uplifted. We all had something to look forward to and the children were excited. A few days before the festive day there was much singing and whispering. The older children cut down boughs of holly and mistletoe to decorate the house. It was lovely to have some fresh greenery about the place. I told my family that many years ago ancient man believed that by decorating the bushes in winter time they could make them attractive for spirits, which they believed had fled to for shelter from harsh weather. Later people began to take branches into their homes to give warmth and shelter to the spirits of nature, releasing them in early spring when the first buds began to appear on the trees. Over time the custom was used to celebrate the birth of Christ. Holly was popular for its brightly coloured berries and mistletoe for its contrasting white berries. Dorothy Howard said she remembered her mother telling her that during Cromwell's time of puritan government he had made it an offence to celebrate Christmas and soldiers even went round town and city houses to make sure that the population were not breaking the rules by decorating their homes with what we would consider to be inoffensive natural foliage. But now it was usual to make a Holy Bough by twining evergreens around a double hoop of willow or other pliable wood and decorating it with something bright such as ribbons, nuts and fruits. When our symbolic Christmas wreath was made, as was the custom, we should have taken it to Church to have it blessed by the parson, Joseph Nichols, in a special ceremony, but we could not get there. I hoped that perhaps he would manage to get up from Baslow to see John at some stage. Nonetheless, we hung our Holy Bough from a beam just inside the front door and any visitors who came during the festive season (if they could get here) would be embraced as a sign that all bad feeling and enmity, if there had been any, was forgotten.

Two days before Christmas, John's brother, Thomas, the shoulders of his cloak covered in snowflakes, arrived laden with parcels – he had even brought a pack animal to carry everything. The horses had waded up from Bubnell through the snow; it wouldn't have been possible to bring a cart. The children were banished from the big hall to the room where Catherine and Elizabeth had their spinning wheels and loom, whilst Christopher and I took delivery of everything. I could see John propping his weak frame up against the doorway of the little parlour and, now a rare thing, a huge grin spread across his lined and worn face as he watched the proceedings. I was given strict instructions not to look at anything until Christmas morning, with the exception that widow Broomhead had sent some sweetmeats and oranges for each of us; she had remembered how I had admired the beautiful decorated fruits at the wedding feast for Thomas and Elizabeth. I don't know how she had managed to get such luxuries for us. I would put them on the table as decoration with the best apples and pears that I had so carefully stored. I thought, with a pang of envy, of the three of them spending Christmas at Bubnell Hall, with so much space but, as yet there were no happy children to run around. Had my husband not been ill perhaps we would all have been able to visit, but it wasn't to be. Perhaps widow Broomhead had thought that too and that is why she had sent us gifts. She must have been sad not to have had any children of her own, but hopefully, her niece would soon have some babies. After removing his damp cloak and warming himself by the fire, Thomas, not bothered about the snow, decided to stay for a few hours with John, and I left them to enjoy each other's company, helped along with a few cider brandies.

But I could not wait for Christmas morning, so when everyone was in bed on Christmas Eve I took out the parcels and placed them round the table and created my central decoration of fruit, nuts and leaves. There were marzipan sweets and gingerbreads which I put on the dresser. I must have been filled with just as much pleasurable anticipation as my children. Tomorrow I would be up very early as there was much to do. I quietly went into the small parlour, now John's bedroom. I did not want to wake him but wanted to make sure that he was reasonably comfortable. His breathing rattled in his chest and I quietly knelt by the side of the bed to gently stroke his eyebrows and kiss his closed eyelids – something my little children always loved me to do when they were in bed at night. But he stirred and opened his eyes and smiled at me. I think we both knew that this would be his last Christmas and I held him in my arms before he drifted off to sleep again and I then eventually crept upstairs to the comfort of the big four poster bed.

***

In the spring of 1713 Elizabeth, now aged seventeen years, has a young man in her life. John is grumpy about it but I remind him that I was only eighteen when we married. Eventually, it transpires that someone else in the family is not at all happy about the romance. I have heard a disturbance outside and go to investigate. Elizabeth is sobbing. Christopher has a cut lip and a swollen eye.

"Found her in the hay with that young whippersnapper Ed Froggatt from Calver way. Don't want him round here….. told him to clear off."

It looks as if he did more than tell him to clear off. Oh dear, oh dear, as if I haven't enough troubles. I tell them both to come in quietly, not to disturb John. I tell them to clean themselves up and I will deal with them both later. This needs handling very tactfully, especially Christopher's hitherto unseen display of, what I can only think is, jealousy. How blind I have been. It will be exceedingly difficult to manage this situation. Neither of them can be sent away. They are both needed here at Woodhouse and Christopher must learn that Elizabeth, or any of his nieces for that matter, are not his property. Later on Elizabeth tells me that she has decided not to see young Mr Froggatt again and she feels she led him on just a teeny bit but had no intention of misbehaving. She wanted to show him the new foal and that's why they were in the barn. At least, thank goodness for that. I was worrying that I had neglected my parental duties and not brought her up properly. Nonetheless, I shall have to keep my eye on her.

***

That year the summer disappeared; I have no recollection of it.

***

It was John's last attempt to climb the stairs. "The hearts" he gasped.

# CHAPTER TWELVE

## 1713, The Will

A few days following John's funeral, Richard Oddy came to visit. At the sight of him I was completely overwhelmed, burst into tears and sobbed as he put his arm round my shoulders and saying "I would like to help you, if I may. Perhaps you would like to go out for a while. Get Christopher to ride with you round the lanes and I will stay here and amuse your children." Dorothy Howard and Jess were there anyway and so it was an acceptable gesture. I went alone. I walked through the chestnut wood at the back of the house, not noticing if my skirts got caught and snagged on the brambles that crowded over the footpath, no longer used very much. Up the steep side of the escarpment, grasping hold of whatever I could to steady me and up to the edge, Gardom's Edge. I was breathless at the top. Carefully I picked my way between the gritstone boulders, not keeping to the regular route up there; I did not want to be seen; wanted to be alone. Eventually I found a damaged millstone, one that had chipped near to completion, and sat down on the slightly rounded surface. This was the top of the world. I could see everywhere and everything for miles and miles, to my left across to Pilsley where my parents live, to Bubnell Cliff and a little further to the right, Hassop and far beyond to distant hills, and down below to Woodhouse and the farm, the fields, Gardom fields. I could just pick out the sheep grazing and see cattle in the yard. I looked heavenwards to the white billowing clouds. Where was John?

To say that I felt confused was an understatement. It wasn't just my emotional state, but the reading of the will and the codicil had clarified my status in the Gardom family. Yes, I knew the terms were customary with rules of primogeniture, but I now understood that the bulk of the estate was to be held in trust for our eldest son, Chris, until he reached the age of twenty one years (he was now thirteen). Woodhouse, its contents, the farm, lands, together with certain life provisions and bequests plus any remaining leaseholds belonging to the Duke of Rutland were to come to me, only if I remained in widowhood. I would lose everything on remarriage. Trusts and legacies had been made for the remaining seven children which they would each inherit at the age of twenty three years; John's brothers Thomas and William and his friends William Barker of Edensor and Edward Heathcoat of Bubnell, were appointed as guardians for them with instructions that suitable apprenticeships were to be found for the boys. Furthermore he gave his afore mentioned two brothers and two friends the remaining equity of all the tenement lands and workshop in Edensor which he held by lease of his Grace the Most Noble William of Devonshire together with land in the possession of widow Brimley and other pastures in Edensor.

There was no mention in the will of John's younger brother, Christopher. There was no provision for him. He was not present at the reading, and I was unable, for now, to tell him.

Due to my fragile state of mind I felt affronted when the lawyer's arrogant assistant came to make the inventory of household goods on 12th December. Much to my relief my brother-in-law, Tom, was a more appropriate candidate assisting with the valuation of livestock and machinery, workshop contents and whatever else was deemed necessary.

Probate was not granted until June 16th, 1714.

***

The good news was that Kate and Sam produced a healthy son, Henry.

***

I heard that Queen Anne had died at Kensington palace on August 1st. Towards the end of her life the poor lady suffered so badly from gout that she could hardly walk. On her death her body had swollen so large that she was buried in an almost square coffin. The Act of Settlement in 1701 ensured Protestant succession to the throne, and George of Hanover would become our new monarch.

***

My six years old daughter, Ann, went to stay for a couple of days with her cousins at Edensor, as she often did. Elspeth Greensmith was a similar age, the youngest child in my brother's family by some years; they were good little friends. I was getting myself strong again and spent as much time as possible outside with the children during the unusually clement winter weather which had been outstandingly dry for months. William Grundy was calling regularly to see Elizabeth. I warned her to moderate her behaviour with her new beau, especially when Christopher was around, but fortunately he had plenty to occupy him with the farm. I thought he was working hard and making a great success of it. How would I eventually tell him that it all belonged to his nephew? For as long as I remained at Woodhouse, he would be alright, that is until my son became twenty one. Would he be content as manager for Chris? Somehow I did not think so.

Richard Oddy often took the boys out with him on various short assignments. He never behaved in an over familiar way with me; I was not ready for it. Would I ever be? What was the attraction for him? Elizabeth and Catherine were learning to drive the pony and trap. We still had the lovely carriage and although it didn't get used much these days I was reluctant to part with it. Dorothy Howard, now a widow like me, Mrs Briggs and Jess were still valuable members of my household. I depended on them and we were comfortable with one another. Somehow, by whatever means required, I would keep them with me, unless, of course, Jess was to marry.

My dishevelled sister-in-law brought Ann home by pony and cart in time for Christmas. She looked very grubby, like a little ragamuffin, but my little girl had obviously had a lovely time. A few days later the child developed a fever. Jess had heard that there was a measles outbreak so we immediately isolated her from the other children. Sure enough little spots appeared on the insides of her cheeks, then a rash developed from the top of her head all the way down her little body. She had painful, red watery eyes, runny nose and eventually a hacking cough. I was beside myself with worry and used every possible recipe from my herbal to try and alleviate her symptoms. I was desperate; what could I do? The fever was very high. My dear littler daughter, Ann, died in my arms in the night. I think my inconsolable wailing could be heard as far as Derby.

The death and burial of one's child is the most terrible, heart wrenching, soul destroying experience. But I had to keep strong for the rest of my young family.

William came all the way from Whitwell and with his brother Tom he supported me. We took the little coffin ourselves in the splendid carriage, slowly down to St. Anne's Church. I could not bear to let her go, to see her gently laid in the same grave as her still born sister and on top of her father and grandfather on the 29th December, in the year 1714.

***

We had chosen the site well, close to the wood. The ground was rich and fertile and the big chestnut trees would protect them. One of the gardeners from Chatsworth House brought them in his cart and planted them for us: four walnut trees. It was a simple memorial that the children, Christopher and I would always remember. I thought of them all: my new born baby daughter who had experienced no life at all, my father-in-law, Thomas Gardom who had taught me so much and although he had lost his wife which was not an uncommon occurrence, had been well looked after by me and had always had his children and grandchildren around him, Anna, my happy six year old child snatched away too soon and my hard working blacksmith husband, John.

***

The sad news reached me that my sister's husband, dear Sam Watson, had died of a seizure and the funeral was to take place on March 31st, 1715. Unable to face any more grief at that time I did not go to Heanor, but my brother attended and I knew that, somehow, James Thornhill would be there. On his return, Edward sent word to me that Kate was carrying a child due to be born in a few weeks' time.

# CHAPTER THIRTEEN

## Spring 1715, A New Beginning

Seeking a rare opportunity for solitude I had gone far across the fields in the vain hope of finding spring flowering twigs for the copper jug or some early primroses which sometimes nestled in the craggy boundary walls. Richard had arrived unexpectedly at the house and Dorothy Howard had pointed him in the direction that she had seen me go. As he reached me thunder boomed, lightning flashed, the heavens opened……. it was pouring with rain. We ran for cover to the nearest place - an old field barn still half full with hay and straw. He removed my wet cloak, gently held my shoulders and his deep blue eyes gazed down on my face. Our hair and clothes were soaked. He didn't take advantage of me. He gently touched my lips with his. My dress slipped off. I was willing, very willing and I pulled him down on me, yielding my body to his caresses and kisses in complete and utter abandonment. I did not want the torrential rain or his love making to stop. The smell and taste of him intoxicated me. The feel of his lean muscular body readily weakened me. There was no going back now; we could make one another very happy. I could not get enough of him. We had both waited long enough but the storm passed over all too quickly.

On our way, slowly and lingeringly, hand in hand, back to the house Richard suggested that he ask permission of my children to marry me "You will, won't you?"

"Is that why you came today?" I replied.

"Yes."

"But what about my children?"

"You don't think we would abandon them do you?"

"We cannot live here at Woodhouse"

"I would not want to. I have made tentative plans in the hope that you will say yes."

"Richard, I think you know the answer."

"Yes."

Before he left us that day, Richard said to me "be ready tomorrow. There is somewhere I want to take you, a house I think you might like."

Our wedding day was arranged for Monday, April 15th. We would then be taking up residence in our new home in Bubnell and I had just a little time to furnish the house and make it comfortable; Richard said that I could please myself.

My life was proceeding at an exciting pace. Richard had whisked me away from Woodhouse on his sturdy Cleveland Bay and for a while I had not a care in the world as I clung to him from my pillion seat savouring every moment and sense of the exhilarating experience. As we rode along Bubnell lane I noticed that the well-made even stoned road was so unlike the rough and often muddy track from Woodhouse and when we reached Bubnell Hall I remembered the first time I had seen the beautiful twin gabled house with its magnificent windows of the banqueting hall and its many chimneys, but of course I had now known for a long time that I could not live there. We continued our journey along the lane following the course of the river, past one or two little cottages and their outbuildings. Richard told me that the occupants would be very willing to work for us. The river now took a completely different direction away from us and I could see below the road tidy little vegetable gardens beautifully laid out in the fertile riverside meadow. It was a long time since I had made this journey and I had forgotten about the house that I now saw - a solidly built stone two storey. It looked so pretty, standing quietly there as if time had stood still. As he slowly lifted me down from his powerful horse Richard told me that there were no incumbents and no furniture! Due to his increasing frailty a certain gentleman, John Broomhead, a widower, had decided to vacate his substantial property for us and had gone to live further up the lane at Bubnell Hall with his sister-in-law, widow Broomhead, who was still of good strength in mind and body and his daughter Elizabeth and her husband, my brother-in-law, Tom Gardom. A nearby stable and some hay were easily found, then, hand in hand, we entered the empty house through the heavy oak door and walked round the timber screen which separated the front door from the body of the room. This was a good sized hall with a large stone fireplace. Although the paintwork was peeling I could see that the walls had been a lovely warm terracotta colour. Richard agreed that it would be most appropriate to renew it. To one end of the hall through a stone archway was a lobby and rising from this the main staircase with well-worn banisters, splat balustrades and acorn-shaped newels. The tall staircase window shed light on both floors. Also reached from the lobby was the beautifully panelled parlour, with ornamented cornices and the fireplace had a handsome timber overmantle set with flower shaped carvings. From the other end of the hall through an archway that Richard explained to me was built of blocks of ashlar stone was the huge kitchen with its magnificent inglenook fireplace, complete with sways and roasting spits. I knew that we would be spending a lot of time in this room. Richard said that he would see that the fire was lit, in the now cold hearth, as soon as possible to get some warmth into the house. There was a good sized bread oven but he said that in future I could get freshly baked bread every day just down the lane in the village. What a luxury, I thought, and I realized that my life was going to be a lot easier than living off the beaten track up at Woodhouse. The house was bigger than I thought with one wing at right angles to the main building. Off the kitchen were the usual scullery, pantries, storerooms, outhouses and privy. "We don't need to make ale either" Richard was saying "we can get what we want from the Baslow ale house." Upstairs there were an adequate number of well-proportioned rooms for us all. I especially liked the room above the parlour as it had a very pretty stone fireplace. "Shall we have this bedroom, Richard?" I asked as he embraced me and whispered in my ear "Good job there isn't a bed in here yet!" We had another look round the house, the good range of outside buildings and then discovered the entrance to an undercroft beneath the house which afforded much storage space. "Oh, this is useful" said my husband to be. "It looks very old, probably two or three hundred years and it's a wonderful place for livestock to shelter in winters of severely cold weather." Almost as an afterthought he added "the warmth from their bodies would keep the house warm too."

Before we left he said "So, will it suit you?" but my beaming face must have already told him the answer: "I think it is perfect!"

As Richard was taking on my children and agreeing to bring them up as his own until they each became of age to receive their inheritance, I had absolutely no qualms about slightly adapting the terms of John's will to suit the circumstances! All the goods and chattels that I wanted from Woodhouse, including the carriage and a pair of ponies, would go with us to our new home. I had heard that some of the furniture at Haddon Hall was to be sold and fancied buying an important looking chair for Richard. I thought it was right and proper that he should have his own chair at the head of the table. During my marriage to John, as was the custom, I never had any money of my own but now, and for the time being, I had my own purse! A couple of days later Elizabeth and I managed to see the caretaker at Haddon and purchased a beautifully carved walnut armchair with turned legs and the high back and seat caned as had been the fashion for a few years. There were several items I would have liked but hoped I could return with Richard if we found we needed further pieces of furniture. But for now I thought he probably had enough to think about.

Naturally, my children were very curious about what was to be our new home and a few days before the wedding we all piled into the carriage; Richard, upfront with Chris, took us to see the house so that they could choose their bedrooms. Their shouts and laughter echoed through the empty house as they scampered up the stairs, rushing from room to room to see which was best. I think they were very pleased. They had something on which to focus, a different place to explore and hopefully the sadness of recent years at Woodhouse would eventually fade into the distance. Jess was to come with us, but her mother, Dorothy Howard, said, understandably, that it was too far for her to travel, besides she did not want to come with us because her life had always been at Woodhouse and she wished to remain in her little cottage if that could be arranged. Somehow I would have to replace Mrs Briggs but I imagined that it would not be difficult living so close to a thriving village. Whether I could find someone as hard working as her would be a different matter!

My daughter, Elizabeth, was to be married to William Grundy on July 16th when they would then be able to move into a little cottage in Bubnell Lane.

***

We had returned to collect more household items. The trustees were with Christopher in the now sparsely furnished little parlour at Woodhouse. It was enough for me to hear Edward Heathcote say "You know, Christopher, at the age of twenty six years it's high time that you made your own way in the world. We are obliged to manage the estate until John's eldest son becomes of age. You can stay on as ..........." I did not want to hear any more.

# CHAPTER FOURTEEN

**Bubnell Old Hall, 15th April 1715**

I am in a state of euphoria. We are walking along Bubnell Lane, alongside the river, to our new home, after our marriage this morning at St Anne's Church in Baslow. The Church holds so many memories for me, most of them sad, but today's events have eclipsed them all for the time being. There are no sad faces today. Our family from both sides are with us and the children have gaily skipped and frolicked ahead of us. It was meant to be a quiet wedding but we have been joined by villagers, those not working, who have turned out to wish us well in our new life together, Richard and me; Richard and Anna Oddy. Even the bell ringers managed a short peel for us before and after the service. I am wearing a beautiful new forget-me-not blue fine woollen dress which Elizabeth and Catherine have made for me. It is still fashionable to wear an under bodice. I know my waistline has spread a little after producing all those babies and I begged my daughters not to lace it too tightly, but it is so uncomfortable and I can't wait to get the wretched garment off. There are tiny seed pearls stitched around the neckline (not too low) of the dress and I have a matching cloak with a stiffened stand up collar. My daughters helped me to dress and swept my fair hair up to my crown, with ringlets clustered at the back and pink apple blossom pinned in securely. I do not wear earrings as I have been afraid to have my ears pierced. Henry VIII had pierced ears; I wonder if they were all infected like his poor gigantic ulcerated legs. I wear no jewellery except now the wide gold ring which Richard gave to me in church. Yes, I am wearing shoes! My handsome husband, Richard, is not wearing his London clothes, is quite plainly dressed; he does not need adornment. What does it matter what we are wearing; it is our day and we are going to enjoy it. For a while the sound of the weir drowns out any conversation or laughter. The children have stopped to see the darting movements of the brown trout as they seem to fly out of the water. Even the fish have joined in our merriment!

Eventually we reach the house. I see that the grassy area at the side has been cut short; trestle tables and bench seats have been set up and there are flagons of wine and ale; the local inn keeper is doing a fine job for us and, at our request, the village baker has cooked a pig and some little fowls. The path has been strewn with blossom picked from the nearby orchard and the heavy oak door is open. Richard carries me over the threshold into our marital home. People may think that this is a marriage of convenience but I already adore him. I hear sweet music and see that a gentleman is playing a viol in the hall. I wonder how much music was played in this historical old house years ago, home of the Bassets, but which has been quiet for so many recent years. Undoubtedly, Richard and I will bring it back to life. Perhaps, in time, the old walls will reveal their secrets.

It seems that almost everyone we know has been unable to stay away and guests have brought us gifts. I am so touched that residents from the cottages have made felt table mats for us; how novel and useful. I wonder if the idea will catch on. The Duke has sent us a haunch of venison from his deer park, a rare treat for us as we are not allowed to hunt the deer. Ezra has brought us some of his lovely honey and I see that he has come with Dorothy Howard. Someone else has brought us a basket of brown hen eggs and there is a pair of beautiful little ornamental fowls in a wooden cage. My sister Kate is not here but William Barker has been to Heanor to see her. When she has finished with it she wants us to have the cradle that Sam made. She thinks he would have been pleased about that. I think how presumptuous she is that we might need a cradle, but, on the other hand, she could be right! William Barker, a good family friend and such a delightful gentleman, is telling me that he is gently trying to persuade her to come back nearer to Baslow where her family live and I tell him that I would be so pleased if that were possible. Furthermore, I suspect from the way he looks when he is telling me this that he feels a great deal of affection for her. The Broomheads have given us a wonderful tapestry; I already know where I would like it to be hung in the hall. Everyone is so kind. There are more gifts to look at, and guests to mingle with but William Gardom, is saying something to me as I am peeping at a whole locally made cheese wrapped in linen:

"Where is my young brother, Christopher? I saw him outside the church on his mare but he doesn't seem to have followed on here."

"Don't worry." I reply. "The ewes are about to start lambing and I expect he has gone to check on them. I'm sure he'll be along later."

My husband, Richard, comes across the room with a beautifully painted wooden panel from Richard Thornhill. He could not come to the wedding as he has such a big project in Greenwich at the Royal Naval College, but if he can manage to visit us when his gout is not too painful he would like to paint our portraits. How wonderful!

Richard's parents are here and have very generously given us a pair of silver goblets. Richard is their only child and not only has he taken on all my children but they have acquired ready-made grandchildren. They say there is something for the children which has been in their family for some time and is rather precious. It is a bestiary, a compendium of amazingly coloured pictures of animals – real and imaginary. We think we will find a quiet time later with the children to look at such a treasure but for the time being will keep it safely in the small parlour.

There is much merriment and laughter, lots of good food and wine. We are surrounded by family and friends. The children are happy. It is a good day and I have a lot to be thankful for.

***

**Tuesday, 16th April.**

I am in a deep slumber dreaming of a rider on horse-back fast approaching.

"Wake up Anna." Richard is rousing me from my dreams. Perhaps I needed a deep sleep after all the events and excitement of the previous day.

"Anna, throw a shawl round your shoulders and come down stairs quickly." There is urgency in his voice.

"Are the children alright?" I ask him.

"Yes, yes, they are having breakfast. Follow me. Come outside." I do as I am bid.

I wasn't dreaming. We have a visitor; I don't know his name but remember seeing him outside the church yesterday:

"I have ridden as fast as I could. From the village we can see smoke rising from beneath Gardom's Edge, from Woodhouse. I thought you should know."

From where we are in Bubnell the hill behind Baslow and the ancient burial mound atop obliterate our view but we can just see beyond that there is grey smoke rising to the sky.

"Richard. Oh no....... Woodhouse. What shall we do?" I feel as if my legs will give way from beneath me.

"Anna, you and the children must stay here and keep busy. There is nothing you can do for now. I am going immediately to Tom Gardom at Bubnell Hall. I hope to catch William before he returns to Whitwell and we will go to Woodhouse. Be brave, my love. Thank goodness you and the children are here with me."

In a matter of moments he fetched and mounted his huge bay horse and, with our messenger, was gone.

I followed Richard's instructions whilst trying not to think the worst scenario about Woodhouse, the home we had only just left. I set about preparing a meal from the beautiful meats left over from the wedding feast; my children were always ravenous and they all wanted to help. We baked potatoes in their jackets in the ashes, there were some tasty pickles and freshly made butter. It would be our first family meal together in Bubnell Old Hall; it would certainly be memorable and it was good for me to have something to occupy my troubled mind. Our feast was laid on the big kitchen table when Richard eventually returned.

It must have felt strange for him sitting at the head of the table with his readymade family. He suggested we drank some wine from our new goblets. The smell of freshly baked bread wafted through the house and would be delicious with the cheese. Needless to say, we could hardly contain ourselves waiting for him to tell us the news.

"I'm afraid the house is burnt to the ground. Some of the buildings are damaged and we cannot tell what caused the fire, whether it was accidental or deliberate. Mercifully all the livestock had been turned out from the farmyard into the fields" he grimly told us.

"Did you see Christopher? Is he all right?" I asked.

"There was no sign of Christopher, or his mare. It looks as if he has gone, but where to, is anybody's guess. We are not to worry; Tom and William Gardom will take care of everything."

This was such an unexpected trauma at the start of our marriage and I wondered how we would ever get over it with so many unanswered questions, but I was determined not to dwell on the matter nor let it spoil our happiness. I expressed my thoughts clearly. "Our life is here with you now, Richard, here at Bubnell Old Hall, not at Woodhouse. There is so much for us all to explore and discover. The future awaits us!"

***

# EPILOGUE

Twelve months later, Anna gave birth to her last child, a healthy boy and he was christened Richard.

Anna's sister, Kate, widow of Sam Watson married William Barker, gentleman of Edensor.

Anna's daughter, Elizabeth married William Grundy on July 16th, 1715 and Catherine married Thomas Alsop in 1721.

Anna's son Christopher married Elizabeth Hadshead in 1724, but sadly Christopher died in March 1726 just before his son, Thomas, was born in April of that year. But his issue thrived (Thomas Williams Gardom) and were still farming at the end of the 1800's at Far End living at The Yeld Farm which had been built against the new Sheffield Road around 1803. Another descendant, John Williams Gardom, became a crepe silk manufacturer. A recent descendant was The Honourable Garde Basil Gardom (1924 – 2013) who was the 26th Lieutenant Governor of British Columbia and was the agent general for British Columbia in London, England.

Johannes did indeed carry on his father's trade of artistic blacksmithing. He married first, Hanna Heathcote who died in childbirth and their daughter died 6 months later. Johannes then married Mary with whom he had several children and their son, John of Bawkes also carried on the family business of blacksmithing in Baslow and Edensor.

Sarah, the great grand-daughter of John and Anna Gardom caused a scandal in the Edensor family when she became involved with nobility and in 1785 gave birth to an illegitimate son.

Thomas became a cooper and married Susanna Poynton in 1729.

There is no record of Maria who was born in 1711.

A William Gardom married Elizabeth Lenthall at Whittington in 1754 and there is a record of William Gardom of Cutthope (O. Brampton) buried in 1794.

John Gardom's brother, Thomas, who married Elizabeth Broomhead, was the father of Jonathan Gardom, who, with John Pares, built the cotton mill at Calver. Jonathan's daughter Elizabeth married, in 1785, James Longsdon of Little Longstone where the family still live.

The names of Martha and Elizabeth Greensmith are fictitious.

John Gardom's youngest brother, Christopher, seems to have disappeared.

# ACKNOWLEDGEMENTS

**Information gleaned from:**

England under the Stuarts by G M Trevelyan

Illustrated English Social History (Volume Two)
by G M Trevelyan

Explaining the Forge by Francis Evans

Historic Food by Ivan Day

British Listed Buildings – English Heritage

A Biographical Dictionary of Sculptors in Britain, 1660-1851 from the Henry Moore Foundation and the Paul Mellon Centre

Derbyshire lead mining history from Wikipedia

Facts about Louis Cheron from Wikipedia

Facts about Antonio Verrio from The Free Library

Facts about Sir James Thornhill from Tate

I am grateful to Dr David Dalrymple-Smith for taking me with my daughter to Gardom's Edge, to my husband, Duncan and to Janet and Louise for their help and encouragement.